Forever Yours

Forever Yours

Forever Yours

Forever Yours

Forever Yours

© Copyright 2021 Kathryn Reign

All rights reserved. No part of this publication may be reproduced, distributed, or transmitted in any form or by any means, including photocopying, recording, or other electronic or mechanical methods, without the prior written permission of the publisher, except in the case of brief quotations embodied in critical reviews and certain other non-commercial uses permitted by copyright law.

Any references to historical events, real people, or real places are used fictitiously. Names, characters, and places are products of the author's imagination.

Cover Design by Temptation Creations (Quirah Casey)

Table of Contents

Table of Contents

Table of Contents

Table of Contents

Table of Contents

Table of Contents

Prologue

I f I had known back then that I would fall victim to hands roughened from laboring in the fields, I would have never left home. Getting into my dream school had seemed like the perfect escape from my routine life. I would move away from my childhood home and become someone else entirely. I would be unrecognizable, a chance to escape the life I'd always hated as a kid.

When I was seventeen, I thought that it was the perfect plan. It all made sense. My boyfriend at the time, one who swore to love me forever, and I would move away. We would pack all of our belongings into a van and spend the summer before college traveling across the country, seeing all the wonders of the country, from major cities to national parks. We would arrive at school, and our lives would begin.

How wrong I had been back then.

I'm thirty-two now. Some would call me smarter, though I would think that was a bit of a stretch. I wasn't smart then, not even now.

Why? Because I still love him.

After years of being free from the domestic abuse, I am still in love with my abuser. Perhaps that is the most disturbing part of my story. After all that he did to me over the years. After all that he continues to do to me. There is still a part of my broken heart that loves him.

Many of us hear of domestic or relationship abuse and immediately blame the victims for not getting out. Why not just break up with them and leave? Why not just walk away? There's no chain attaching the two of you. You have feet; just walk out the door.

And I can see why you might be thinking that. It's a lot easier to see the flaws and horrors of domestic abuse when you're not physically in the relationship. It's easy to see with objective lens that there is no love or future in domestic abusive relationships, especially when children aren't involved.

But I stayed. Looking back, outside of the abuse, I still can't understand how I let it get so bad, how I let an innocent date become a deadly relationship, and how I made an excuse for one punch that opened the door to many others. Was I stupid? Was I too foolish and naïve to know someone's hitting me when their fist was in my face? Was I so desperate to keep a relationship that I just excused every shitty action my partner was committing? What's wrong with me? I never thought I would become a face of domestic abuse, a statistic, but here I am, raw, unfiltered, and exposed.

Back then, I tried to leave. More than once. I knew that the situation was never going to improve. There were times that I thought I would die at his hands. It's funny how abusers never start off as your potential killer. Not once in those first few dates did I think that he would wrap his hands around my neck and threaten to end my life.

Of course, the relationship lasted less than a year.

How does someone go from the person you are madly in love with to the monster hiding in your closet within the span of a few months?

It was a thought that I had grappled with for the last several years. How do you love a man and hate him at the same time? How did he become the man who stalked my nightmares? There was no clear answer to any of it.

By now, I thought that I would be over the feelings. The terror. Little did I know back then that this man would plague me for years to come. There are times that I wish I could go back in time and not meet him. Not allow him into my life. Yet, there are also times that I would gladly relive all the good parts of the relationship all over again.

Day

1

One

There was nothing better in this world than the tub of chocolate chip ice cream I clutched as Lauren scrolled through my phone. She grinned and swiped rapidly. I didn't want to know who she was liking. Instead, I reached for the glass of wine beside me and took a sip. If only there were enough wine to drown my problems with.

Lauren rolled over and tossed the phone beside me, a picture of an average-looking man facing up.

"You need to stop this wallowing, Natalie. You and Josh broke up like six months ago. He was a loser, anyway. Remember all those times he cheated on you and stood you up?"

I sighed and turned down the volume on the television. "It's not just that."

"But it *is* at least that." Lauren sat up on the couch, leaning back into the cushions with a sigh. "I don't know what else we can do to get you over him besides getting you under someone else."

"We were together for five years. Then out of nowhere, he dumped me! We started dating when we were sixteen. It's hard to let something like that go. I thought he was the one. We had talked about getting married and having kids. There was a whole future planned together. Hell, we even escaped our shitty childhood hometown together. We connected on so many levels, and I don't think I can ever find someone like that again."

"Which is precisely why we are scrolling through dating apps and looking for the perfect one-night stand."

Lauren handed me the phone. With a roll of my eyes, I took it and started looking through the profiles she had liked for me. None of them had anything in common with Josh. Maybe that was the point. Although, there *was* something to be said about Josh. We had our problems, but he had always been amazing.

He walked into my life at the lowest point. My parents were never around much, but when they were, I was tossed around like I was nothing, a no one. I spent hours each morning trying to cover bruises or tape up broken fingers and toes. There would be endless nights of picking broken glass out of my wounds. Stitching together pieces of skin.

There were times when things were good. When I believed that my parents loved me. It wasn't until I was older and with Josh that I understood what love really was. He changed everything for me. He was the person that I cared about the most. For a long time, nothing mattered but him. There was nothing that could come between us.

He came into my world and tore it to shreds like a hurricane reaching the shore. Nothing was left in his wake. We graduated high school, packed all of our things into a van, and moved to a different state. Starting school put a strain on our relationship, but it didn't last long. We were more in love than ever and ready to start the rest of our lives together.

Last year, we ended up moving back home with my parents to save money for the wedding. Everything was perfect with him. It made sense. I was never going to find that in another person.

"Earth to Natalie. You spaced out on me again."

I shook my head and smiled at Lauren. "Sorry. I was just thinking about all the things that could have been. You realize my life is ruined now, right? I had plans. Plans that were made with him in mind."

"Well, he's gone now. However, the man that is on your screen right now is looking pretty good. He's only a couple years older. And he likes cooking. You like cooking. He likes hiking. You like hiking. It sounds like the perfect match."

I laughed and shook my head. "If I send him a message, will that get you to lay off about this?"

She shrugged. "For now. I have other comments to make on your life, though."

"Naturally."

She grinned and closed her eyes, tilting her head back against the cushion. With a roll of my eyes again, I clicked the message button. To be fair, the guy *was* attractive. Josh had been cute, in that boyish kind of way, but this man was something else entirely. He had a dark shadow of stubble along his jaw and dark hair that fell into his eyes. I could also see a hint of tattoos peeking over his collar.

He definitely isn't ugly, I thought as my thumbs hovered over the keyboard. *But what the hell am I supposed to say to him?*

I had never done this before. Josh and I met in high school. That's how everyone met back then. Now, there were tons of apps and different ways to meet people. How was I supposed to know what to message him?

Caleb: Hey there, I saw that you like hiking. I have to know, where is your favorite place to hike?

I read the message through again. Before I had the chance to think of something, he sent the message first. Now, I was stuck trying to figure out how to keep the conversation going. Sure, I loved hiking, but picking my favorite spot was always a difficult task. Josh and I spent the entire last summer going from National Park to National Park. Some of them were great, but others were down near the bottom of my list. There were other places that I would want to go a thousand times before I went back to one particular place.

"Just pick a place!" Lauren said, her breath on my neck.

I yelped and tossed the ice cream, jerking away from her. I didn't realize that she was that close. Clutching my heart, I looked at her. "Are you *trying* to give me a heart attack?"

"Maybe a little bit. But seriously, it's not that hard to respond to the man. You love that little park near here with the tiny waterfall."

"It is not a tiny waterfall."

"Anything that Josh showed you was tiny."

Grinning, I elbowed her. "You're stupid."

"You love me."

"Kind of have to. You're my best friend."

She nodded. "And as your best friend, I'm telling you that you have to message him back."

Natalie: I like Whitman State Park.

Caleb: Whitman is nice. I thought there was a waterfall there, but I haven't found it yet.

Natalie: There IS a waterfall! I can't tell you how many nights I've spent camping near that waterfall. It really is pretty. You'll have to find it someday. It's off of the trail and toward the back of the park. It takes probably another two hours of walking, but it's so worth it!

Caleb: Maybe you could take me there sometime?

Natalie: And how do I know that you aren't some crazy murderer?

Caleb: I guess you're just going to have to take that chance. Kidding! You have my full name and my picture. You can stalk me all you want online. I promise I won't do anything that involves murdering you. Although, I really think we should go on a date. There is no getting to know people properly through these apps.

Natalie: I don't know...

There were still some slight murderer vibes.

"What the hell are you on about?" Lauren asked as she snatched my phone. "You need to stop acting like some little girl and agree to go on a date with this delicious man. Seriously! Get over Josh."

"What are you typing?"

She stood up and held the phone out of my reach. I stood up, trying to grab it from her, but she was good at keeping the phone away from me. When I jumped, she dodged and moved out of my way. With a laugh, Lauren hit the send button.

"There. Now, you have a date set. Tomorrow. Noon. He's going to meet you there."

I groaned as I sat back down on the couch and buried my face in my hands. "What the hell did you just do?"

"I'm helping you get over your ex. You have a date with Caleb McCord tomorrow at noon. I expect you to go on it and have a little bit of fun. You deserve it after so long."

Peeking through my fingers, I scowled. There was a sinking feeling in my stomach. Nothing could compare to the relationship that Josh and I once had. What would be the point in even trying again? There was none, as far as I was concerned. Yet, there was something about this man, Caleb, that made me think there might be something worth it. I could try talking to him longer, get a better feel for who he was. There were other things that we could talk about, though I didn't know what. I was never good at getting to know people in relationships. Josh had been my first and only boyfriend.

"You look like you're overthinking everything. You need to calm down. Nothing bad is going to happen. You know that, right? He's just a guy, and you're just a girl. Together, you are going to go on a nice date. At the end of the date, you'll come home. Do you know what happens after that?"

"I die of mortification?"

Lauren laughed and shook her head. "No. If it was a good date, you agree to another. If it was a terrible date, you never talk to him again. Simple."

"Easy enough," I said sarcastically as I reached for the ice cream tub on the floor. "There are many other things that I would rather do with my Saturday."

"Just give this guy a chance. Something really great could come out of it."

With a sigh, I settled back against the cushions and clutched the ice cream once more. "Fine. I'll give him *one* chance, but I'm not giving him anymore than that. I've seen all the idiots that *you* bring around. I don't need one of those, too."

Lauren grinned as she curled up with a pillow beside me. "Uncalled for, but definitely fair."

And that was that. I'd go on the date and give Caleb a chance. What's the worst that could happen?

Forever Yours

Day

2

Two

Caleb: Good morning! We still on for our date today?

I stared up at the ceiling for a few more minutes, trying to think of what to say. There was a huge part of me that wanted to tell him we would have to postpone. If I did that, we would never reschedule. Then I'd have Lauren in my face once again about needing to get under somebody.

Natalie: Hey, definitely! Still noon, right?

Caleb: Yeah. I was thinking that we meet in the parking lot on Branson Street.

Natalie: Sounds good.

Caleb: I have to admit. I'm a little nervous. You're so beautiful, and it has been too long since I went on my last date.

Natalie: I know the feeling. I had a horrible breakup about six months ago, and I'm just now trying to get back out there. It's kind of a weird feeling. I never thought I would date anyone else, you know?

Caleb: I know what you mean. My wife died two years ago, and I haven't been able to bring myself to really try dating again until now.

I sat up and rearranged my pillows before settling back down. There was still another two hours before I had to get ready to go out. Now was as good a time as any to try and get to know Caleb. It might make the date easier, in a sense. At least, there would be something to talk about. More insight into his interests.

Rolling over, I dropped my face into my pillows and groaned. This was ridiculous. I was a grown woman. I wanted to love somebody, and I wanted to be loved by them. That would require me going on a date with this man. After another moment of wallowing in my desperation, I finally texted back.

Natalie: I'm sorry to hear that. How long were you married?

Caleb: Almost seven years. Got married the day she turned eighteen, and we never looked back.

Natalie: Do you have any children?

Caleb: No. Neither one of us wanted them. Enough about my old life now, though. I feel like I'm going to bore you with talk about the man I used to be.

Natalie: What do you want to talk about then?

Caleb: Tell me about you. I saw on your profile that you are still in school.

Natalie: For another few months. After that, I get my teaching degree.

Caleb: Where are you going to work? Dream school maybe?

Natalie: I wish. Right now, I think I'll just end up teaching in an elementary school.

Caleb: Well, Natalie, I'm going to have to let you go for now. I have an anxious dog that needs walking, and my sister will kill me if she finds out that I didn't take him out today. Sadly, the dog is the only nephew I am getting from her.

Natalie: Good luck! I'll see you later!

I tossed the phone off to the side and got out of bed. Stretching, I heard the pops of my spine as I reached toward the ceiling. After a moment of holding the stretch, I walked out of my room and down the hall. There was humming coming from the kitchen, and the smell of pancakes wafting my way. With a grin, I entered the kitchen and took a seat at the island.

"You look happy," Mom said as she put a plate of pancakes in front of me. "It's been a while since I've seen that smile."

"I have a date today," I said while I grabbed my knife and fork.

There was silence for a minute, the room only filled with the sound of my knife against the plate as I cut my pancakes into little squares.

"What do you mean?"

I looked up at her with a sly grin. "What I mean is that I am going to Whitman State Park with a man who wants to spend time getting to know me."

Her hand stilled over the pan; the spatula frozen in midair. "I thought you were still hoping for another chance with Josh."

"Yeah, that's not gonna happen. He dumped me for no reason six months ago, remember? Ghosted me, treated me like I was trash? If he still wanted me, he would have come back by now. I'm done waiting around for him. All I'm doing is wasting my time when Lauren thinks I should be moving on."

Mom's frown deepened as she flipped another pancake. "I thought I saw her sneaking out of your window last night. You know that she can use the door, right? You guys have been friends since you were in diapers."

I shrugged. Mom said nothing else. Instead, lighting a cigarette and pushing aside a bottle of stale beer. With a sigh, I ate my breakfast quickly. The moment of brief care she had for me was gone as quickly as it had come. I thought that things would change after Josh had moved out. Maybe my mother would care more about me after watching me go through my first heartbreak. I had been wrong, though. While there were brief moments where she acted like a mother, they were few and far between. When I was younger, I would spend hours in my room crying about her naturally cold demeanor. Now, it was easier to understand that I couldn't make my mother love me, no matter how hard I tried.

The moment I was finished with my breakfast, I raced back upstairs and showered. Once I was clean, and my hair had been styled in two thick braids, I pulled on a pair of black skinny jeans and a flowing top. When I approached the vanity, my hand hovered over the makeup.

Do I put any on?

Josh used to say that I looked better without it. I thought that he was full of shit back then, too. This was a new man that I was going out with. I wanted to impress him. What if he liked girls who wore makeup? What if he hated them?

"Put on some damn makeup, and call it a day," I muttered to myself as I picked up the mascara.

After applying my makeup, I looked in the mirror. The girl staring back at me looked like a deer caught in headlights. I could feel the sweat on my palms as I wiped them down on my jeans. This was not how I had imagined my weekend going. I thought that Lauren and I would spend the weekend watching movies and studying together. Instead, I was going out on a date with a man I just started talking to.

I didn't recognize the girl in the mirror. She was something that I had never seen before. She was single and free. Was she ready to settle down again? Hell no.

For the longest time, I thought Josh and I were going to get married. We moved in with my family to start saving money for the wedding. In a matter of a few months, he dumped me. There were no signs. No warnings. One day he was there, and the next, he was gone, not even a trace or remnant left over.

"Enough," I said as I stepped away from the mirror and went to grab my phone. "You are going on this date, and you are likely going to have a good time. Josh is gone now. Deal with it."

There was a thump on the wall, followed by my father's grunt. With a scowl, I grabbed my purse and car keys. The date wasn't for a couple more hours, but I had to get out of this house. Without a roommate, there was no way I could afford to live outside of my parents' house, especially in this economy. I would have to do something soon, though. Living in this house for most of my life had me fearful of ending up like them. I didn't want that. I wanted to be free. To do as I pleased. To not have constant reminders of how much of a burden I was.

The back door slammed behind me as I left the house and headed to the ancient truck I drove. It was unreliable at best, but between tuition and student loans, a new car was just out of the question.

When the key turned in the ignition, the engine sputtered before dying. Cursing under my breath, I turned the key again. Another sputter. Another death. I slammed my hand against the dashboard, uttering a few curse words before turning the key again. Finally, the engine roared to life.

"Good girl," I said as I rubbed the dashboard with a smile.

The radio played tunes from decades ago while I drove down the dirt driveway that led to the main road. Dust flew up behind me as I sped toward my freedom. Just a few years ago, I had driven a van down this very same road with my entire life packed away inside it. Now, I was back in the same home, and the life I thought I had slipped through my fingers.

I turned up the radio and put on my sunglasses. It was a bright and warm day, spring taking away the last of the winter chill. It would only be a matter of months before I graduated school and was on the path to a new life. Thinking about the freedom I would gain once I was done lifted my spirits slightly.

Singing along with the radio, I drove down the winding road toward town. There had to be something that I could do in town to kill a couple of hours. As I drove, I drummed my fingers on the steering wheel, the open windows whipping my hair back and forth. There was something about spring and the last frost melting away that made me feel like life was finally starting to look up.

When I got to town, I parked outside a little café. My phone was buzzing on the seat beside me. I picked it up and scrolled through the notifications before I saw Caleb's name.

Caleb: Hey, can we push the date until next weekend? My sister's dog got hurt on the trails, and it looks like I'm spending the rest of the day at the emergency vet in the city.

Natalie: Sure. Next Saturday?

Caleb: Perfect. I have to go now, but I'll talk to you later.

I slipped the phone into the back pocket of my jeans, my heart sinking in my chest a bit. Maybe he didn't even want to go on the date in the first place. It was possible. Lord knows that Lauren was pushy. She had set up the date in less than five minutes. Maybe he felt like he was obligated to go because I had asked. It would make sense. He wasn't over his dead wife, and I wasn't over being dumped. There was nothing that made sense about us going on that date.

I walked into the café and placed my order before taking a seat at a table in the corner. Now that my date was cancelled, I would have to find another way to occupy my time. Lauren was busy at work, which left me to my own devices. There were things I had to do around the house, but those were best done when my parents were wrapped in another drunken stupor. If I got in their way, something would be thrown at my head.

"Hey, your order, ma'am?"

I looked up at a young man with bright blue eyes clutching my coffee. He placed it down on the table in front of me before walking away with a smile. There was something about him that reminded me of Josh. I shook my head and grabbed my coffee.

I'm done thinking about that ass, I told myself over and over again as I sipped at the hot coffee. For the time being, it was my mantra. I would get over it one way or another.

"Oh my god, Natalie Grace? I didn't know you were back in town!"

I looked up, trying to find the source of the shrill voice. When I did, I found myself wishing that I hadn't. "Hey, Bea, how are you?"

She flounced over, heels clacking against the floor. The legs of the chair scraped against the floor as Bea dragged it out to sit down. "I've seen Josh around, but I didn't know you were back, too. How are you guys doing?"

Gritting my teeth together, I forced a smile. She knew exactly how we were doing. She was just hellbent on hearing me confirm her greatest wish. I wouldn't be surprised if she was already sleeping with him. Bea had tried sinking her claws into Josh all throughout our last year of high school despite knowing I was with him. Hell, I wouldn't be surprised if she slept with him the day after he dumped me.

"We broke up awhile ago."

She plastered on a smile that was as fake as her chest. "I'm sorry to hear that! You know what they say, though. There are always more fish in the sea. I think you'll find someone again soon."

"Thanks."

She stood up and smoothed out her skirt. "It was great catching up with you, Nat! We'll have to do this again sometime soon. The girls will be thrilled to hear that you're back."

"I've been back for the past year," I muttered under my breath as she walked away.

Deep within my pocket, my phone started buzzing.

Caleb: Hey there. Sorry I had to cancel. Still at the vet. How do you feel about me calling you later? I really would like to get to know you a bit more before our date. You seem like an interesting person, and you are definitely cute. It'll be nice to hear your voice. You know, make sure you're not a dude.

Natalie: Lol. I would like that.

Caleb: I'll call you when I get home then.

With a grin, I slapped five bucks on the table and ran out to the truck. I had to be ready for when he called.

The next morning, I stumbled down the stairs close to noon. Mom was sitting on the couch with a cigarette hanging from her lips. As I walked by, she looked up and flicked the ashes onto the carpet.

"Who were you talking to all last night? You kept your father and I up. How are we supposed to work and put a roof over your head when we have to call in sick due to exhaustion?"

I rolled my eyes and kept walking. "I don't know. I'm sorry. I was talking to that guy I was supposed to go out with yesterday.

The couch groaned as she got up. I took a seat at the kitchen island and hoped that she wouldn't come in here. The last thing I needed was my mother bothering me after the wonderful night I had. Caleb and I talked from just after dinner until the sun came back up. He was like nothing I had imagined. Never before had I laughed so hard or spilled my secrets to someone I had just met. It was as if there were a connection there. Something that had been missing with Josh. That most basic level of understanding each other.

"What's he like?" Mom walked in and leaned against the counter; her arms crossed.

"He's interested in me, and I'm interested in him. That's all you need to know about him."

She smashed the burning end of the cigarette into the counter.

"I don't like this. You're attached to a man you haven't even met. Last night, you were telling him everything about your life. Don't you think that's weird to share without even meeting him first?"

"No."

Mom sighed and shook her head. "Are you stupid? You're going to get yourself hurt. Or worse, killed. Do you think that I like having to be the one who says 'I told you so' all the time? Maybe if you listened to me every now and then, you wouldn't end up getting hurt as much."

"You're just upset that there's somebody out there who sees me as worthwhile. You and I both know that you wish you had given me up for adoption."

The returning smile and nod were cruel. It felt like a knife ripping through my chest, though I knew it was the truth. She and Dad wished that I had been given up for adoption. It wasn't a secret in our family. Mom felt as if she had missed the best years of her life because of me, and she had been sure to let me know it at every turn.

"You're damn right. But that doesn't mean I want to see you come home crying again over another stupid boy. They aren't worth your time."

"I think that may be the first piece of motherly advice you have ever given me."

She shook her head and left the room. "Don't say I didn't warn you."

Day

7

Seven

Whitman State Park was beautiful on sunny days. Bright green light filtered through the thick canopy of leaves. Dogs and their owners were running up and down the dirt trails. Children were laughing and playing while their parents walked slowly behind them, savoring the last drops of coffee in their cups.

I had always liked going to Whitman State Park. There was something soothing about walking along the trails before stepping off of them to go explore the other open areas the park had to offer. It was a place where I could be entirely alone with my thoughts, where I could clear my heard and work through whatever had been bothering me that day.

Standing in the parking lot waiting for Caleb, however, was less soothing. Over the past week, there hadn't been a single night where we didn't stay up until the early hours of the morning talking. We would text each other throughout the day, even while I was at school. It made focusing on lessons nearly impossible, but there was just something about him that drew me in like a moth to the flame. He was smart and funny. Kind without reason. There was a passion for life that I had never seen. Caleb McCord was intoxicating.

"Hey, there you are," a deep voice said.

I turned around, and my breath caught in my throat. Standing in front of me was the man that, until now, had only existed in my phone. Now, here he was, and he was so much better looking than the pictures I had seen.

"Hey."

He had a crooked smile on as he leaned against the tailgate of the truck.

"Getting shy on me?"

I laughed, the sound definitely stemming from nerves.

"A little bit. Yeah. This is all new and kind of weird, honestly."

"I know what you mean. We'll take it slow, though."

Nodding, I looked toward the entrance of the park.

"How about we stroll down the shorter of the two trails? It goes by the lake."

"Sounds good to me."

Together, we entered the park. The dirt trail was soft beneath my feet, leaves crunching as I walked. Hesitantly, I looked over at Caleb and felt my cheeks heat up. He was far more attractive than his pictures had depicted, and I couldn't stop staring at him. The shadow of stubble and dark hair were both perfectly groomed. Swirls of black tattoos crept down his arms and up his neck. Somehow, it looked good on him. In the past, I had never been a fan of tattoos, but on Caleb, I was turning into a massive fan.

"You're staring," he said, the lopsided grin appearing again as he looked down at me. "Do I have something on my face?"

My cheeks were on fire. "No. Sorry. I was just looking at your tattoos."

"And what's the verdict?"

"They suit you."

He laughed, the sound echoing off the little cliff beside us. "You know, I have heard a lot of things about my tattoos, but I don't think anyone has ever said that they suit me before. I'm not sure if I should take that as a compliment or not."

"It's definitely a compliment."

He nodded, considering it for a moment. "Alright. If you say so. Now, I have questions for you."

"Like what?"

I looked up at the hazy green light that came through the leaves. Birds were chirping, and there was a squirrel jumping from one branch to the next. Looking back at Caleb, I could tell he was studying me. He slowly looked me over, as if there was something specific he was searching for. I didn't know if he found it or not, but he nodded to himself and looked ahead once more.

"Why did you come back to town? From what you've told me, it seemed like you were dying to get out your entire life."

"My fiancé and I wanted to save for a wedding at the time. It made sense to switch schools and move back in with my parents so we could do that."

Little did I know, it wouldn't last long. I wish that I had known. If I had known how things were going to turn out between us, I would have refused to move back home. I would have stayed exactly where I was.

"So, he wasn't just your boyfriend then?"

I sighed and ran a hand through my hair. "Yes and no. We were engaged, but we never told any of our friends or family. It seemed like it would get too messy if they knew the full truth of what was going on with us. My family isn't exactly the most supportive."

"That sounds like their loss then."

"They never wanted me to begin with. It's no real loss, honestly."

We fell into another comfortable silence as we walked. He grinned at me as his hand wrapped around mine. His callouses were rough against my hand, but in a way that felt familiar, like I had been holding his hand all my life. It was a comforting touch, the kind of touch that I knew I would seek when things got rough.

"Does it scare you?" I asked as I looked at him. "Feeling this way for someone else?"

"What way would that be?" he replied, his voice low as he stopped and turned to face me.

The blush returned in full force as I averted my gaze. "I don't know. Maybe it's just me, but I feel like I've known you my entire life."

He reached up, a finger tracing my jaw and stopping beneath my chin. Caleb tilted my face up, and our eyes locked. My heart was hammering in my chest as he stared at me. After a moment, he leaned in. His lips were soft against mine as butterflies erupted in my stomach. I stood on my toes, my arms wrapping around his neck. He pulled me infinitely closer in the middle of the path. It was then that I knew, that in his arms was where I belonged.

When he pulled away, there was a small smile on his face. My cheeks felt impossibly warm as the smile twisted into that lopsided grin.

"It's not just you."

Day
12
Twelve

Caleb had become the first thought in my mind when I woke up in the mornings, and the last person I talked to before I went to bed at nights. Since our first date, we had spent nearly every free moment together. He would pick me up for school and drive me home after. In Caleb's mind, my truck was unsafe and not suitable for driving into the city. I thought he was just being overprotective, but I wasn't going to say no to spending more time with him. It was an hour each way. That was two hours in the run of the day that I might not have had if he wasn't driving me around.

"What are you thinking about?" Caleb asked as he drove down the highway toward my campus. "You look like something is on your mind."

"Just thinking about how surreal everything is right now," I said with a smile as I looked down at our linked hands on the center console. "Did you think that when we matched on that stupid app that we would still be seeing each other almost two weeks later?"

He grinned and pulled my hand over to kiss the back of it. "I'll be honest. I wasn't sure that you would even like me. You're five years younger, and you are way out of my league."

Laughing, I rolled my eyes. "There is no way that I am out of your league. Not even a little bit."

We were quiet for a few minutes before he finally spoke again.

"I know you said that things are getting really bad at home again."

I nodded. Things *were* getting bad at home. For whatever reason, seeing Caleb had ignited a fire within my mother. Every day when I came home, she seemed to be on a new warpath. Everything, from the way I breathed to the way I hid in my room, annoyed her. I had been called every name under the sun and then some. The only time that she wasn't pissed off at me was when she was too drunk to care.

When my father jumped in, it got worse. Dodge the bottle was my new favorite game. From the moment I walked in to the moment I made it to my bedroom, there was abuse coming at me from every angle.

"You could definitely say that things have gotten bad," I said while running my hand through my hair. Turning away from him, I looked out the window at the trees that blurred as Caleb raced down the highway. "I don't know what to do anymore. Pressure just keeps building up at every angle. Pretty soon, things are going to explode."

"Well, I *have* been thinking about a solution to that problem."

"Oh, have you now?"

There was a teasing tone to my voice, but I was worried. When I was living at home, there was only so much abuse that I would be able to take before I left again. This time, I didn't have anyone to fall back on. Lauren was still living with her parents, and they hated me, seeing me as a bad influence for her. I couldn't afford to live on my own, either. Until I graduated and got a job, I would be stuck.

"Yeah, I have, and I think that I might have found a solution."

I scoffed and took my hand from his, crossing my arms.

"I really don't want to talk about this right now, Caleb. Can we talk about literally anything else?"

"No. I think we need to talk about this. Now. I think you're in danger, living with them. I want to keep you safe and protect you, Natalie. I know we just met, but I'm falling for you, hard. I'm not going to risk letting them ruin the best thing that has ever happened to me."

Heat rose in my cheeks, but I shook my head. "Well, there's nothing that we can do about it. Nothing at all. We may as well stop talking about it."

"If you would just let me talk to you for a minute," he said, reaching out to ruffle my hair. I batted his hands away and smoothed my hair back down. "I have a house. A big and empty house that could use someone other than me living there. I know that it's still really early in our relationship, but I know, without a doubt, that I'm all in. I hope that you are, too. That's why I was wondering if you wanted to move in with me."

I paused for a moment, not quite sure of what to say. It seemed like a big step so early on in our relationship. We had only met twelve days ago, though it seemed like a lifetime had been spent together already. It would solve the problems I was currently having at home. There was also our relationship to consider. I was sure that I was in love with him, too. Or, if I wasn't yet, it would only be a matter of a few days before I became head-over-heels.

"Are you sure? I mean, you haven't known me that long. I could be some kind of crazy murderer who is just waiting for a chance to get inside your home and kill you. Sell some body parts for money. That kind of thing."

He laughed. "There is no way that you are that kind of person. And of course, I am sure. If I wasn't certain of my feelings for you and where I think this relationship is going, I wouldn't have made the offer. I think that you and I could be very good together. Incredibly good, actually. I haven't felt this way for anyone ever. Not even for my wife when she was alive. You are something else entirely, Natalie."

I was at a loss for words. I didn't think that there was anything I could say to that. There was something between us, something deeper than I had felt with Josh. It was a sense of belonging. A sense of being sure that the relationship with Caleb would last forever.

"If you're sure you want me to move in," I started to say before he grinned the lopsided grin that always made my heart melt. "People are going to say that it's too soon, though. They are going to think that we're moving too fast. Possibly making a mistake."

"Do *you* think that we are making a mistake?" The grin faded quickly, turning into a deep scowl. "Do you think that choosing to move in with me would be a mistake? Or maybe you think that our entire relationship is going to be a mistake? Tell me now, Natalie, so I know if we're wasting our time or not. I'm too old to be screwing around with a bunch of what ifs."

Running a hand through my hair again, I sighed. "It's not like that at all, Caleb. I have to worry about what my parents will do. You know that."

"Why do you have to worry about what they'll think? You're an adult. You can make your own choices, and there's nothing that they can do about it if they don't like them."

"There is plenty that they can do. A ton of things. They can ruin our lives if they really wanted to."

He pulled up into the parking lot at my school. "Look, we'll talk about this tomorrow, okay? I can't pick you up after school today."

"Then why the hell did you drive me?" I snapped as I grabbed my backpack and got out. "How the hell am I supposed to get home?"

He reached over to slam my door shut before pulling into an empty parking space. When he got out, he walked over and handed me the keys. "Drive yourself home. My sister will come and pick me up here."

"Oh. Um. Thanks," I said, feeling like an ass for snapping at him. I should have known better. He wouldn't abandon me an hour from my home with nobody to pick me up. "I'm sorry I went from zero to a hundred. I should have known that you weren't just going to leave me here."

"Of course not," he said as he pulled me into a hug. "I'll see you tomorrow, okay? I love you."

"Okay." I didn't know what else to say. Did I love him? I didn't know.

After a brief kiss, I ran toward my class. I was already late, and my professor was not one who would tolerate tardiness.

When I got home with Caleb's car, the fighting had already started. When I announced that I would be moving out, my parents were surprisingly happy. Dad had ranted about one less mouth to feed and one less person to clean up after. Of course, it was usually me who cleaned up after them, but I wasn't going to start anything that didn't need to be ignited. Shit only hit the fan when I mentioned who I would be moving in with.

"What are you talking about?" my mother shouted as she followed me out of the living room and into the kitchen. "You can't move in with a man you just met. I know you're not the smartest person out there, but I thought you were at least smarter than *that*."

"I'm a grown woman, Mom. I can make my own decisions. Living here isn't working out for any of us. Caleb has offered me a place to stay."

Mom scoffed and leaned against the counter, sweeping a beer bottle out of the way. "And what does this man – who is older than you – want in return for letting you stay in his home? I'm sure he wants something."

"I don't think he wants anything other than a relationship with me. You're being ridiculous. There is nothing bad that's going to come of this. Not at all. I want out of this house, and you want me out, too. Why are you so pissed off about me making both of us happy? You no longer have a daughter that you don't love, living in your home, and I'm free to do as I please."

"You are a stupid fool if you think that moving in with this predator is going to be good for you!"

My face burned hot as I lost my words. I stared at her for a moment before shaking my head and walking toward the stairs.

"Anything will be better than living here."

Day
20
Twenty

I smiled as the sun streamed in through the window and across my face. It had taken nearly a week to pack all of my things and pull the rest out of storage. Now, I was ready to move. Caleb would be working all day, but he had given me the key yesterday. Last night, I thought I wouldn't start moving until the afternoon, but all it took were a few moments of hearing the screaming downstairs before I was out of bed and heading to my decrepit truck with a box tucked under one arm.

"Where do you think you're going?" Mom asked.

She was sitting on the front porch, one foot dangling over the hole in the planks while a stub of a cigarette hung out from the corner of her mouth.

"Moving in with Caleb today. I told you that." I threw the box into the bed of the truck. "What's it to you anyways?"

"You know what? Go ahead and ruin your life like I ruined mine. Maybe then, you'll realize what I went through all these years to keep a roof over your head and food in your mouth."

"What about when I needed my mother? What were you doing then? You were off working or at the club with your friends. You didn't give a shit about me. Don't pretend that you ever did."

Without another word, I charged back into the house and up to my room. Grabbing as many things as I could, I made the trip back to the truck. When I got outside, my mother was gone. I shrugged off the feeling of disappointment that I felt.

Even though I was sure of my decision to move in with Caleb, sure of his love for me, there was a part of me that wanted my mother to tell me not to do it. I wanted my mother to act like she cared for me, like what happened in my life mattered to her. By now, I should have known that it didn't, but there was still hope. A little piece of hope clinging onto a cliff of despair.

As I sat behind the wheel of the truck, I took another look at my childhood home. For years, it had been a place where I was free to do as I wanted, for better or for worse. Nobody cared whether I was home or not. There was nobody telling me what was right or wrong. My parents never cared about me.

I backed the truck down the driveway. I was heading toward my future. Toward someone who cared about me. Someone who loved me for me.

Saying Caleb's house was large would be an understatement. Though I didn't have many things, it was hard to see what aspect of me would be represented in the home. He had an entire life already set up, and I was just being planted there.

I wandered through the house, finding more than one extra bedroom and a couple of bathrooms. The kitchen was bigger than the entire first floor of my house. Though he had never told me what he did for a living, it had to have paid well.

Finally, I found the master bedroom. Windows stretched from floor to ceiling along one wall, with thick curtains hanging on either side. The windows overlooked a massive backyard with a pool in the middle. I grinned, already thinking of the days that I would spend in the warm water.

After finding the second walk-in closet, I started hanging up my clothes. There was far more room in the closet than I would ever need, but it was nice.

When I finally graduated, I would be able to have an entire wall just for my work clothes.

Grinning, I left the closet and grabbed a book. It was time to spend some time lazing by the pool and enjoying the sun.

I hadn't been outside long before my phone started ringing. Caleb's name flashed across the screen, and a smile threatened to split my face in half.

"Hey," I said as I answered the phone. "I hope you don't mind, but I got an early start moving. Your house is absolutely stunning, now that I've seen it in the daylight."

He laughed, the sound low and warm. "Our house, babe. Look, I'm calling because I'm going to be running a little late this evening. I had also planned on stopping at the grocery store on my way home, and now I don't have time. Do you mind going for me?"

"Not at all. Did you have a list ready?"

There was that laugh again. Butterflies fluttered in my stomach. "Not even close to a list. Normally, I'd just go and let things find their way into my cart."

"I'm sure I can manage."

"You're the best."

"I know. I'll see you when you get home?"

"See you then, babe."

When I got home that night with the groceries in tow, the lights were off. There was soft music coming from the study. Caleb must be home. Turning on the lights, I put all of the groceries away in a hurry. It had been a long and lonely day, and I was ready for us to enjoy living together.

Opening the study door, I was shocked. There was a woman, naked and splayed over a desk while Caleb sat in the chair behind it. A cigarette was pressed between his lips, and a thin curve of smoke rose toward the ceiling.

Without a second thought, I walked into the room and grabbed the woman by the hair.

"If you know what's good for you, you'll get the hell out of my house in the next five seconds."

After giving her hair a hard yank and snapping her head against the table, I let her go and crossed my arms. There was a hooded look to Caleb's eyes, and a small smile was twisting his mouth upward. The woman scrambled to gather her clothes before racing out of the room.

"What the hell do you think you're doing?" I asked, my voice low and dangerous. "It's ten o'clock at night. You told me you were working late."

The smile dropped from his face as he stood up. His shirt was missing, but at least his boxers were still on. He put the cigarette out in a little ashtray and stepped around the desk toward me.

"Babe, nothing happened."

I scoffed and took a step back. "Do I look stupid to you? If nothing happened, you'd be wearing clothes, and there wouldn't be some naked woman on your desk."

"Look, she's crazy."

Tears blurred my vision as I took another step back. "Who the hell *is* she?"

"My ex-girlfriend. Look, babe, she came over here while I was working on a project proposal. She got undressed and onto the desk before I could say anything to stop her. I promise, babe, I was already undressed before she came over. I had no clue that she was going to do that."

"Weren't you with your wife for the last seven years?" Rapidly, I tried to blink away the tears. "Where in that time would you have had time to find a girlfriend?"

"She was around before I met my wife." He shook his head and frowned. "That doesn't matter anymore. You're here. It's only you I love, darling."

"I don't believe you." I shook my head and wiped away the tears that were sliding down my cheeks. "You're a jackass. I can't believe I thought that something like what we have would ever be real. It's all been nothing but a big lie. All of it. Not a single word of anything that you have ever said to me has been true, has it?"

In less than a second, he was across the room, and I felt the sting of a hand against my cheek as my head snapped to the side. The sound echoed through the room, the final nail in the coffin for that night.

"Get out of my house," he said, the words nearly a growl. "Get the hell out of my house, and never come back. How dare you accuse me of something like that?"

I walked out of the room, my steps slow and hesitant at first, until I finally turned and ran. My cheek was on fire, and my ego was bruised. Wrenching open the door to the truck, I climbed inside and locked the doors. It was only then that the panic set in.

He hit me. How could he hit me?

It felt like nothing had changed. Like I hadn't left my home to escape the abuse at all.

As I watched the house, I saw the light turn on through the upstairs window. The window flew open and moments later, clothing started flying out of it. I watched as my belongings headed toward the ground, where the sprinklers were in the process of turning the yard into a mud puddle.

With my stomach tossing and turning, I wiped my tears once more, wincing as I touched my bruised cheek. After a moment, I turned the key in the ignition and left behind the future I thought that I had.

My mother had been surprised to see me. As always, she was seated in front of the house, consuming packs of cigarettes. I ignored her as I walked into the house with what little I had left. My mother trailed behind me, making the house reek of whatever she was smoking.

"Why are you back?" the woman inquired.

"It's none of your business."

That was a mistake, though. My father, who had been sitting in front of the TV, heard me and slammed the clicker on the table. He had a cigarette between his lips, too.

"You will *not* talk to your mother that way!" he yelled.

I rolled my eyes and continued to make my way toward my room. But my mother wasn't going to have it. I hated it when she was this way. I preferred when she stayed out of my business.

"You're going to give me an answer, Natalie!" she demanded. "Why aren't you with that Prince Charming of yours?"

"Because I got tired of staying there," I responded.

My mother scoffed. "That's a fucking lie!" Then she moved forward and touched my cheek, exactly where Caleb had slapped me. I pushed her hand away.

"He hurt you," my mother added.

I heard my father chuckle. "She's got a sharp mouth. The dude must hate it."

My eyes began to gather tears again. I didn't want to cry in front of these people. The last time I did that was five years ago.

"That doesn't give him the right to touch her," my mother defended. "Who the fuck does he think he is?"

I was surprised to hear her say that. My mother had hurt me, but why she was behaving like she actually cared was beyond my scope of knowledge. I let out an inaudible hiss and went into my room, slamming the door shut behind me. My mind had yet to believe that Caleb had hurt me, that he was cheating on me with another woman. Why was he acting like this?

My phone buzzed. When I looked at it, it was a text from Caleb. He was asking where I was, all the letters written in caps. I could almost hear him yelling at me. There was no point in talking to him. I just rolled sideways and tried to sleep.

But I couldn't. My phone started ringing. Before I stared at the screen, I already knew who it was. Caleb.

"What?" I barked.

"Babe," he said. "You left."

"I had no choice. You threw me out. What the hell was that?"

"Listen, I'm so sorry about what happened. I wasn't thinking straight. You need to come back home. Forget about what I did."

Somehow, Caleb was talking like a lunatic. Just a few minutes ago, he had thrown my stuff out into the muddy yard. Now, he was asking me to overlook that. His defense was that he wasn't in his right mind. How did that even make sense?

"No, Caleb," I said simply. "Goodbye. Don't call me ever again."

Day
25
Twenty-Five

"Does it look like I've been crying?" I asked Lauren as we walked through the campus parking lot.

"I should put him six feet under."

I shook my head and nudged her shoulder with mine. "Enough. It's over. He's out of my life for good, and I'm busy kissing the ground that my parents walk on so they won't kick me out, too."

"You know that all of this is a horrible idea, right?" Lauren said. "I can offer you a place on my floor for awhile."

"No. It's okay."

I looked over at my truck and saw Caleb leaning against the tailgate. When our gazes locked, he stood a little taller and stuffed his hands into his pockets. Immediately, my stomach began twisting and turning. I wanted to run to him and away from him at the same time.

"Don't even think about it," Lauren said as we stopped at her car. "You are better than some jackass that you barely know."

"I have to talk to him," I said. "I'll see you in class tomorrow, okay?"

She scowled but nodded. "If he hurts you again, he'll have me to deal with."

"I think I can handle this myself, but thanks. I love you."

Caleb shifted his weight from one side to another as I walked over to him. There was a hesitant smile on his face as he reached for me. I stayed just out of arm's length and shook my head.

"What the hell do you want, Caleb?" I clutched my books tighter to my chest, willing myself to be brave. If he were going to do something, he wouldn't do it out here in the open. At least, I hoped that he wouldn't. "Why are you here?"

He sighed and ran a hand through his hair. "I acted like an ass that night. I should have told you the truth, and I never should have hit you. It was in the heat of the moment, and I lost my temper. It will never happen again, babe, I love you. I told you that

I have never felt this way before, for anyone, and I meant it. I don't know what I was thinking, raising my hand to you like that."

"That doesn't change the fact that you did it."

"I know. I shouldn't have. I am sorry, Natalie. I really am. Please. I will do anything to make it up to you. It'll never ever happen again. I love you. I can't live with myself for what I did to you. Please forgive me."

"You hit me. You cheated on me."

"I'm an idiot." He stepped forward, reaching for me again. This time, I allowed him to pull me closer. There was something about him, a magnetic pull, that drew me to him. "I'm never going to hurt you again. Please move back in with me."

"Okay," I whispered, allowing the tears to fall freely.

It had been less than a week, but I did miss him. Now that he was by my side, everything felt right.

The next day, Lauren took me to church. I wasn't the religious type, but I couldn't say no to what she told me after confessing to her that I was ready to go back to Caleb.

"You're possessed," she had said. "That man has taken over your mind. I know how to set you free."

I looked incredulously at her. "Set me free? I'm not trapped."

But Lauren would never accept that. "You don't see it. I do."

Her church was located on campus. It was called the Cathedral of Hope, and the building was so small, anyone would have passed by it without giving it a second glance.

When I got inside, the ceremony had started. The inside was so quiet I wouldn't be surprised if I heard a pin drop. Lauren led me to the last pew in the church and whispered to me to bow my head in prayer.

"Why?" I asked her.

"Because you have to talk to God."

I didn't protest but did as she said. Nothing came to mind. I didn't know what to pray about. Instead, I decided to pray for Caleb. Whatever was bothering him, I asked the Big Guy to take it away from him.

After a few minutes of silent prayer, Lauren tapped me on the shoulder. I raised my head to look at her. She was wearing a smile.

"How do you feel?" she asked.

"Feel?" I asked back. "I don't get it."

But Lauren wasn't impressed. "You're supposed to feel peaceful. What did you really pray about?"

Before I could reply, an elderly man stepped on the altar. He was tall, lanky, and couldn't stop smiling. I believed he wanted to appear friendly to the congregation, but he only looked awkward.

"Praise the Lord," he said.

"Hallelujah," the church chorused.

The once silent church was no longer silent. They seemed happy to see the pastor, or maybe it was the giant cross of Christ behind him. Whatever it was, everyone appeared excited to be here. It was almost as though they radiated peace.

"God will never abandon his own," the pastor continued. "No matter how far we stray from him, he is always there to take us back. I don't know what you're facing, but you need him in your life. He is the only one capable of saving you."

I was starting to get bored. These religious people always claimed this. I really didn't understand how they could depend on an unseen deity to solve their problems. My mother had taken me to church once, but the following Sunday, she stopped going. I had a feeling it was because the minister talked about how hating your children and making them sad were sins. She did that to me. She didn't want to admit it.

This minister wasn't any different from the one in my mother's church. If they could see our pathetic lives, why didn't they try to help us? Why did they expect us to go to some God and ask him for help?

"Okay," I told Lauren. "I have to go."

Lauren grabbed my wrist. "Where exactly do you think you're going? We have to meet the pastor after the sermon. I already told him about you."

"About me?" I was beginning to get angry. "You told him about Caleb?"

Lauren shrugged. "He gives great advice. What else could I have done?"

I took my bag and got on my feet, ignoring the worshippers in front of me turning around to see what was going on. I walked out of the church just as the pastor asked that the congregation rise to pray.

Lauren was behind me. She kept calling my name, but I wasn't ready to talk to her. I was about to leave the church's parking lot when she caught up to me and pulled me around.

"Natalie! Why don't you want to talk to me?"

"Because you have no right to discuss my private life with your pastor!"

"He fucking slapped you!" Lauren tried to defend herself. "I had to tell someone."

Her response did nothing but enrage me even more. Lauren might be my friend, but she knew that respecting my privacy was one of the things that had made us last this long as friends.

"Without telling me?" I yelled. "That's not how friends do things!"

Lauren's eyes turned misty after I said that. I didn't know if my words had hurt her.

"Natalie, I was only trying to help."

I sighed. Maybe I had overreacted. Lauren was only looking out for me. That was what any good friend would've done. I shouldn't have shouted at her.

"Lauren, I'm sorry," I said to her. "But I just don't like the idea of another man knowing about my life. I barely know him."

Lauren sniffled. "He's a good man. That's why I told him everything, and he's very interested in meeting you. Natalie, just talk to him. Let him know what's happening in your life."

I glanced at the entrance of the church. People were already streaming out in twos and threes. The pastor himself was talking to a church member, laughing at something the person had said. Maybe it wouldn't be so bad talking to him after all.

"Okay," I said to Lauren. "But next time you want to tell someone about me, maybe a heads-up first."

Lauren's smile returned. "Of course."

The pastor's office felt warm and inviting when I entered. It had a wooden desk, two office chairs, and an air conditioner that made the air misty cool. The man seemed to have a taste for nature because most of the portraits on his desk were of oceans, waterfalls, and grassy mountains. Only a large Bible on his desk really depicted that he was religious.

"Welcome, Miss Grace," the pastor said. "Take a seat, please."

Lauren had come in with me. Without waiting for me to say anything, she pulled a chair out for me and took the other. I decided to keep a smile on my face as I faced the pastor. It would be rude to make him see that I didn't want this.

"Pastor Cooper," said Lauren. "Thanks for meeting with us."

"Oh, it's nothing," the pastor answered. "Ever since you told me about Miss Grace, I knew we had to meet. Bless God that we are now."

"I'm thrilled." That was me.

If this man really had the spirit of God, then he should have known that I just lied. However, he grinned and opened the Bible on his desk.

"Have you ever been to church, Miss Grace?"

That was a difficult question I didn't want to answer. The last thing I wanted was the pastor trying to convert me. I didn't believe in his God. Why should he force it on me?

"Sometimes."

"Does Caleb go to church?"

To be honest, I knew nothing about him. Caleb didn't look like someone who would want to go to church. In fact, I had never heard him say anything about Christ.

"I don't think so," I told the man.

He looked up at me. "You don't know?"

I stole a glance at Lauren. That was why I was avoiding the meeting. Awkward questions annoyed me.

"He doesn't go to church," I replied.

"Then am I permitted to say you're both living in sin?"

Well, it depended on what he considered a sin. As for me, nothing passed off as iniquity. I was a free person, unlike what Lauren had thought. She was the one in bondage, having to respond to doctrines and biblical principles.

"Pastor Cooper, I assure you that Caleb and I are fine," I told the pastor. "It was just a disagreement."

Pastor Cooper closed his Bible. "Miss Grace, what Caleb did to you isn't normal. You have to understand that."

"Pastor Cooper, couples fight," I insisted. "It's not a big deal."

But the pastor wasn't ready to agree. He opened his Bible again and peered at it.

"Have you ever heard of people being controlled by demonic spirits?"

I leaned in my chair, folding my arms as he said that. "I don't believe in demons. If you're saying Caleb is being controlled by one, you're wrong. He looks fine to me."

"Natalie." That was Lauren. "Maybe you should listen to the pastor."

I decided to keep quiet and let the man of God talk about devils living in people and making them evil.

"Even Jesus recognized these demons and sent them out of people," Pastor Cooper continued. "They are objects of unreasonable characters, of malice, of poor hatred. To me, Caleb is portraying all of these. He needs to find God, or he is going to hurt you in the end."

I didn't want to admit it, but I had thought of it when Caleb slapped me in the room. My head could have hit anything, and that would be my end. But luckily, it hadn't happened.

However, I was sure it wouldn't happen again. Caleb had assured me. He said he was sorry. I wanted to take him by his words.

"He wouldn't do that," I confessed to the pastor. "Caleb loves me. Why would he hurt someone he loves?"

Pastor Cooper's expression had now turned serious. "Your parents love you, don't they?"

I glanced at Lauren in disbelief. "You told him about my parents, too?"

Pastor Cooper jumped in. "Miss Grace, your friend told me because I felt she was troubled by something. I felt it in her spirit."

"That's bullshit," I snapped.

"Natalie!" cried Lauren.

"You know what?" I said, rising to my feet. "I'm done with this! All of this! There is nothing to talk about."

The pastor was studying me, fingers steepled under his chin. "Perhaps, you're the one in need of God."

"Thanks, but I seriously don't need your help," I said, grabbed my bag, and stormed out of the office.

Lauren didn't bother to chase after me this time. She was probably still taking to the pastor or had realized how wrong it was for her to tell him about me.

I wanted to cry as I walked out of the church. Everything hurt me. Being with Caleb had felt like I was finally going to be happy. I didn't have to push it. My time of happiness was bound to come. Not even the Big Guy in Heaven could deny that. Caleb would make me happy. All I had to do was be patient with him.

Yet, I couldn't get the pastor's words out of my mind. What if he was right? What if Caleb's action were just a tip of the iceberg?

That shouldn't be my problem now. I was headed to his home where we would have a long talk. Caleb had to assure me that he wouldn't repeat what he did several days back.

I needed his assurance. I wanted his love.

Day
28
Twenty-Eight

I thought that he would change. I thought that I would mean something to him. That I was enough to be by his side. Instead, I looked like a fool. I didn't bother to throw the woman out this time. Once the bed stopped squeaking, I waited for her to stumble down the stairs, her top half on, and her mascara running down her face. After the door slammed behind her, I marched up the stairs and into our bedroom.

Without a word, I dragged the new clothes Caleb had bought for me – replacements for destroying my old clothes – and packed them into a large suitcase. He said nothing, watching me from a dark corner of the room. Once I set the last shirt in the suitcase, he got off the bed.

"Where do you think you're going?" he asked, his hand closing around my bicep. "Babe, it's late. Why don't we talk about this in the morning?"

Instead of responding, I shook my arm free and disappeared into the bathroom. Gathering my things, I tried to keep my cool. Taking deep breaths, I packed the last of my very few things and zipped the last zipper.

A hand gripped my bicep again, fingers digging into the muscle. "I said, where do you think you're going?"

"Away from you. I should have never believed you. You don't love me. You only love getting what you want."

He paused before his grip tightened once more. "You're not going anywhere. We're going to stay up all night and work through this like adults."

"No!"

My head snapped to the side. He had moved so fast that I hadn't seen it coming. The hand that had been holding my arm lifted when I wasn't looking. He struck me in the same place as last time, the sting twice as painful.

"Get out, then! Run away like the child that you are instead of dealing with your problems!" He sighed and turned away from me. "I love you, but I should have known better. You're young, and you're dumb. You could never love me like I love you. Just go."

I didn't look back as I gathered my things and walked out the door.

Day
35
Thirty-Five

It had been a week, and it felt like I was being eaten alive from the inside out. Caleb wouldn't return any of my calls. Each time I had gone over to apologize, he didn't bother coming to the door. Instead, I was left looking like a fool and losing the only man who had ever loved me this much.

"I don't know what to do," I said to myself as I slumped against his door.

I pulled my knees to my chest, hugging them tight as the rain started to fall. The wind was cold, and there was a storm brewing. Thunder rolled, and lightning flashed. I had never felt like more of an idiot.

The night grew darker as I sat there watching the rain. I couldn't go home without making things right between us. I had overreacted. He had lashed out. It was my fault. I should have listened to his side of what had happened. There would have been more to the story. He loved me. Maybe he had problems with commitment after his wife died. It wouldn't be crazy to think that.

Finally, after what seemed like most of the night had passed, the rain stopped, and the door behind me open. I tumbled backward inside.

"What are you doing here?" Caleb asked, his voice gravelly.

"I wanted to apologize. I acted like a spoiled brat last week, and I should have stayed around to talk it out with you. You lost your wife. You've been going through a lot, and I haven't been the most supportive person. I should have done better. You love me, and I love you. Nothing else should matter, right?"

He sighed and motioned for me to come in once I got to my feet. I followed him into the house and toward the plush couch. Sinking into the cushions, I grabbed the blanket from the back of the couch, pulling it tight around my body.

"I'm sorry."

He sat down on the ottoman across from me. "I don't know if that's good enough. You don't care about me enough to hear my side of the story at all. You jump to conclusions about what happened without any actual evidence."

"I know. It won't happen again."

He sighed and rubbed the stubble on his chin. "I can't deal with this high school bullshit, Natalie. If we are going to be together, I need to know that you are in this for the right reasons. I need to know that you want to be with me, and only me. I need to know that you're going to trust that I am going to do what I think is right. I only have your best interests at heart."

I nodded. "I know. I'm sorry, Caleb. You and I are something more than all of the high school drama."

He was silent for a few minutes before he moved over to the couch, pulling me into a tight hug. "I'm sorry, too. Now, what do you say you go home and get ready to move back in?"

"I'll go back to my parents' and get my things."

My mother was sitting in my room when I got home. The screaming match started as I packed my things and continued until I was back in the truck. I looked in the mirror as I drove away, hoping that I would never have to return.

Caleb was waiting outside when I got back to his house. Beside him were a pile of crushed cigarette butts. His frown was deepening the wrinkles across his forehead.

"Are you alright?"

"No." He sighed and rubbed his forehead. "I lost my job."

"Well," I said as I sat beside him and took his head. "I can go to online school for the last few classes that I have. Do school at night, and I can get a job during the day to help with the bills while you look for something else."

"You don't know how high the mortgage is."

"We'll make it work. I promise."

Day

42

Forty-Two

Caleb still hadn't found a job. In the past week, it had caused more than one fight. I didn't think he was even interested in looking; meanwhile, I had been working two jobs and going to school. Each night, I'd come home more tired than the last, only to head straight to my studies. Caleb was understanding, though. Dinner was always ready by the time I got home. He kept the house clean. There wasn't much more I could ask for.

I seemed to have forgotten that I should be far away from here. His respectable attitude made me forgive him, but the truth was, I don't think I was ever really angry at him. Every time he pinned me to the floor, hammering his knuckles into my face, I wasn't sure I ever hated him for it. Caleb was my man. I had no intention to walk out of his life.

"How are you doing?" Caleb asked as I walked into the kitchen.

There were black and white decorations across the cabinets and through the fake plants. The fancy dishes were on the table, and there were several platters of food in the center.

"What is all this?" I asked before giving him a kiss. "What's the occasion?"

"Well," he said as he reached into the pocket of his jeans.

He pulled out a small black velvet box and got to one knee. I clasped my hand over my mouth, tears welling in my eyes as the butterflies in my stomach went wild.

"What are you doing, Caleb?" I whispered.

"Just let me finish," he said with a grin.

"Are you sure?"

"Natalie, I have been in love with you – head-over-heels, completely in love with you – for the past month. I know that we have had our problems, and that people are going to say we are moving too fast. Maybe we *are* moving fast, but you are the best thing that has ever come into my life. Will you marry me?"

"Absolutely," I said.

His crooked grin was wide and beautiful as he slid the ring onto my finger. I admired it for a minute before he stood and pulled me into a hug. "I love you."

"I love you, too. Now, what do you say we toast to our future?"

He walked over to the champagne and poured two glasses. We raised them high, clinking our flutes together.

Here's to the future, I thought as I stared at the love of my life over the edge of my glass.

Life didn't get much better than this.

That night, I dreamt about our future. It was a perfect feeling I didn't want to ever wake from. Caleb was holding my hands as we raced in a field of green. The air carried our pure love, wrapping us in a golden realm of affection.

"This is amazing, Caleb," I heard myself tell him.

He turned to face me, his eyes radiating his love for me. "It's as amazing as you are."

I blushed, cradling his hand in mine. "This is everything I've ever wished for. Why do we have to fight all the time?"

Caleb brought my face close to his, about to answer, but he was interrupted by the happy cries of some children who had come to meet us. They were three in number: a boy and two girls. The boy looked a lot like Caleb, bearing his dark magical eyes. The girls, on the other hand, smiled the same way I did when I looked in the mirror.

"Mommy!" one of the girls said, running to hug me.

A tear almost dropped from my eye as I returned the hug. She felt so warm and real in my arms. The smaller girl was sniffing my hair. I wanted to hold them forever. The boy had gone to Caleb, standing by him and looking at us.

"The kids miss you, Natalie," said Caleb. "Don't ever leave us."

I blinked back tears, crushed by the guilt of leaving during all the times we fought. I would never do that again. We had kids now, and we had to stay together.

"Let's go home," Caleb spoke, stretching a hand out for me to hold.

Home was my parents' place. I wanted to ask why we were going to them, but just as I opened my mouth to speak, my mom burst through the door, dressed in a pink flowing gown with an apron around it. She was wearing a smile that I had never seen before on her face.

"There they are!" she said. "Come on in!"

When we got inside, dinner was already set. I didn't know why I no longer felt the delight that I had back on the field. My father was there, his own smile creeping me out. How in the world were my parents acting normal?

"Let's eat," my father announced and took my mother's hand.

I didn't move, just rooted in my seat. Even Caleb couldn't take my hand. He was staring at me, waiting for an explanation.

"Natalie, it's time to eat," the voice that came out of Caleb sounded demonic.

When I glanced at him, his friendly smile had vanished, replaced by a deep frown. I knew that expression. I knew what was coming.

"Natalie," my parents chimed. "Eat your dinner!"

Their tone was one of command, equally demonic as Caleb's. With trembling feet, I got up, backing away from them. Like a lightning bolt, Caleb came for me, punching me in the nose. I staggered, banging my head against the wall.

I could hear my children crying, but that didn't dissuade Caleb. He came after me, inflicting pain on me with every move he made. My parents didn't defend me. They egged him on.

My world was falling apart. Nothing was blissful anymore. It was pain upon pain. By the time I woke up, tears were already streaming down my face, coupled with fright that threatened to consume me.

Day
47
Forty-Seven

Five days. The engagement ring was on my finger for five days before I found another woman in my bed. Three different women, all in the span of our relationship.

"Take your stupid ring back!" I screamed as I threw the ring at him while the woman ran out of my bedroom. "You are nothing more than a lying, cheating, son of a bitch!"

He flew out of bed, his hand wrapping around my throat as he slammed me into the wall. The air was knocked from my lungs as I gasped and clawed at his hand. Caleb leaned over me; fury written clear across his face. His breathing was heavy as his hand squeezed my neck tighter.

"Who the hell do you think you're talking to?" he growled as I tried desperately to pry his fingers away from my throat. "Who the hell do you think you're talking to, Natalie? I know that it can't be me because you wouldn't dare disrespect me like that!"

A scream left my body as he tossed me to the side. I was on all fours, gasping for air when his feet appeared in my line of vision. I tried to scramble away, but he continued to advance.

"Do you know what the problem is with our relationship is? It's you. You are never enough to keep me satisfied. You are a prude in every sense of the word. You only have sex with me once a week if I'm lucky. Of course, I am going to go somewhere else to get it."

I screamed as his foot connected with my ribs. As I curled into a little ball on the floor, I whimpered. It was all my fault. He was right. If I was willing to put out more, be the fiancé that he needed, he wouldn't go around chasing after all these other women. It was my fault. Completely and entirely my fault.

"I'm sorry," I whispered as I peeked up at him. Tears streamed down my face. "I am so sorry. You're right. I'm not being the woman you need. Please let me be that woman, Caleb. I love you. Please."

He smiled and crouched down beside me, his hand drifting through my hair.

"It's okay, babe. I forgive you. Now, how about I run you a hot bath and then you come downstairs, and I will make you dinner?"

"Thank you."

I wasn't sure he heard me, but he ducked into the bathroom. I could hear the water running as the tears poured down my face. It was my fault. It was always my fault.

Day
51
Fifty-One

The last time I saw Caleb was four days ago. When he left, we were okay. He was irritated with me still, but he was no longer angry. Instead, he said that there was a job in the next town over that he was going to interview for. I crossed my fingers, hoping that he would be able to get it, and wished him a safe trip. It seemed like the longer he stayed at home with nothing to do, the angrier he got. Living off of the money I made had to be eating away at his pride.

Before Caleb left, he insisted that I invite Lauren over to stay until he got back. Of course, I jumped at the chance to have my best friend with me.

"What do you think you're still doing with him?" Lauren asked on that fourth night. "I can see the bruises under the makeup. Don't you even dare think about lying to me."

"Do we have to talk about that? I thought we were going to work on planning my wedding while you're here."

"I can't believe that you are thinking about getting married to this man, after everything I suspect that he's done to you. You need to stand up for yourself, Natalie. Leave. You can move in with me. I don't want to see something terrible happen to you. Please, come home with me."

"No." I stuck my hand into the bowl of popcorn that sat between us and pulled out a fistful. "I'm not going anywhere. He would never intentionally hurt me, Lauren. I made him upset, and he lashed out. It's not going to happen again. I know now that I wasn't being a good fiancé."

"Do you even hear yourself?" Lauren asked as she shook her head. "I can't believe you're talking like this. Natalie, he is brainwashing you into thinking that everything is your fault when he is an abusive monster."

There was a slam down the hallway. I looked up and saw Caleb standing at the doorway with his luggage at his feet. He glared at Lauren, his nostrils flaring.

"I think it's time for Lauren to leave," Caleb said, his voice low and slow. "Natalie, you and I need to talk."

"What do you mean?" I looked between Lauren and Caleb. "We had a few drinks, babe. I don't think it's safe for her to drive home."

"She can walk. Or I can call the cops to escort her off my property and all the way home. It's her choice."

Lauren looked at me. "Can you believe this, Natalie? Are you really going to let him talk to me like that?"

I frowned and looked at the popcorn I still clutched in one hand. Slowly, I dumped it back into the bowl.

"Lauren, I think it's for the best that you leave. Caleb and I have a lot to talk about."

She shook her head, tears whelming in her eyes as she got to her feet and left. The minute Caleb turned the lock behind her, I felt dread eating away at my stomach. When he came back into the room, his eyes looked as if they were entirely black. My Caleb was not here anymore.

Two steps were all it took for him to cross the room and grab me by the hair. I screamed as he threw me through the glass coffee table. Sharp shards dug into my arms, warm and sticky blood coating my skin and the rug. I tried to get on my feet, but the moment I was up, there was a hand around my neck. Gasping for air, I clawed at his hand, trying to free myself. Black dots danced across my vision, and the world around me started to spin.

Rough brick scraped my back as my head bounced off the mantle. I was in a crumpled heap on the ground, bleeding and battered as Caleb advanced once more.

"I come home from trying to find a job to provide for you, and I find you talking shit about me with your friend? What kind of woman does that?"

Caleb's foot stuck out, landing in the fleshy part of my stomach. I curled around it, my ribs aching, and my breath coming in short, sharp intervals.

His hand closed around my bicep, and he dragged me to my feet. As he hauled me down the hallway, I could still feel the world spinning around me. The door opened, and without a care in the world, he tossed me into the front yard. The door slammed shut as the sprinklers turned on.

After a few moments of trying to breathe through the pain, I pulled my cell phone out of my pocket and dialed the only number I could think of.

"Mom," I whimpered when the call finally connected. "Will you come get me?"

When she arrived, Caleb had already left the house. I was thankful because the last thing I wanted was a face-off between my mother and Caleb. I wasn't sure I knew how that would end. As soon as she found me back in my room, crouched at the foot of my bed and staring at nothing, my mother let out a gasp. I turned to look at her, but her expression quickly turned into a frown.

"Get up," she said. "You look like a mess."

I whimpered, feeling the hot tears run down my cheeks. I couldn't even bring myself to stand up. There was no strength to do it. I wanted to stay in that position forever. However, my mother wasn't going to have it.

"Well, he's clearly a crazy beast," she started, throwing my stuff into a bag. "You need to get as far away from here as soon as possible."

"I thought...thought...he loved me," my lips quivered as I said that.

My mother hissed. "He doesn't. No one who loves you would ever do this to you."

It was ironic that she said that, considering I first knew pain from her. Yet, she would talk about loving me. I didn't know what to believe anymore. Caleb was just like them.

After she finished packing my clothes, my mother came to me and tried pulling me to my feet. I shrieked in pain because she had dug her fingers into my bruises. However, no apology came from my reaction.

"Just get on your feet," she demanded. "I might end up killing that boy if he shows his face here."

That was enough motivation for me to stand. I limped as I followed her into the living room. While we were on the way to her car, my mother passed by an expensive-looking vase sitting on Caleb's mantle. She stopped to study it, then without warning, took it, and smashed it on the floor. The vase shattered like my heart did any time Caleb hurt me.

"Mom!" I exclaimed. "Why did you do that?"

The woman proceeded to his kitchen and started breaking his plates. In no time, Caleb's kitchen appeared as if a herd of bulls had raced through it. My mother had a smile of satisfaction plastered on her face.

"Mom," I groaned.

"No one beats my daughter," she responded. "I wish I could smash all this on his head instead."

"Mom, this is wrong. He's going to hate me."

My mother glared at me. "Are you even listening to yourself? What has he done to you? Did he put you under a spell?"

I shook my head and headed outside, unable to find the correct answer. My mother had no idea how much I loved Caleb. There was no doubt that she had no love for my father. So, how was she supposed to understand me?

"Natalie!" she called after me. "What did he really do to you? This isn't you."

I spun around, suddenly, to look at her, my rage swelling in me.

"You know nothing about me!"

Forever Yours

Day
61
Sixty-One

"If you don't tell that man to get the hell off my property, my gun will," Mom said as she walked into my room. "You and I may not have always seen eye-to-eye, but I will be damned if you go back to that abusive son of a bitch."

"He's not abusive." I got to my feet, limping and holding my ribs as I walked down the stairs.

Going to a doctor was out of the question. They would pry too far into my business, find out who had done this to me. I would not be given a moment's peace, and it would get Caleb in trouble. I couldn't have that. No matter how upset I was, the fight hadn't been his fault. I hadn't defended him against Lauren, and I should have. We were supposed to be getting married, and I had betrayed him.

"Hello," I said as I stepped outside and closed the door behind me.

"I'm sorry, babe. I lost my temper. I should have given you a chance to tell your friend to back off before I jumped in. It wasn't fair. I know that you love me."

"You really hurt me this time, Caleb."

Walking down the steps, I kept my distance, but I wanted to run to him. It had been ten days, and I missed him like crazy.

"I know, honey. It's not going to happen again. I promise. When I get mad, I'll leave. I'll go for a walk or to the gym or something. I don't ever want to hurt you again." Tears were streaming down his face as he got to his knees. "Please, baby. Take me back. Tell me that we can make this right."

"It can't be like the other times, Caleb. You have to mean it this time. I know that I make you upset, but we have to find other ways to work through our problems together. We need to be a team."

"Anything you want, Natalie. Just please say that you will come home with me."

I studied him for a minute before nodding. Being away from him felt as if my heart was being ripped out of my chest. Slowly, I walked over to him and grabbed his hand, waiting until he got to his feet before I pulled him into a hug.

"I'll come home."

That day, I met Caleb's friend, Cole Watkins. He was the first person I had ever met from Caleb's life. Cole Watkins worked at the Federal Penitentiary and had been there for three years now. He was a lively man who spoke of Caleb's good traits. To be honest, he made me love Caleb again.

"We're childhood friends," Cole said as I served him a plate of stir-fry and grilled chicken.

I smiled and took my seat across from him. A gasp escaped from my lips as I did that, but I wasn't sure Cole had heard it. It was a result of the pain in my ribs. Caleb had given me painkillers to do the magic, but the drugs didn't seem to work. The pain was impossible to ignore.

"Are you okay?" Cole asked.

He *had* heard. My eyes stung with tears. I wanted to tell him that I wasn't, but Caleb was looking straight at me. The last thing I wanted to do was embarrass him in front of his childhood friend.

"Sure. I'm fine," I replied and quickly changed the topic. "You were talking about you and Caleb being childhood friends."

"Yes," Cole said, breaking into a grin. "His father was a military man who came to live in my hometown."

I faced Caleb. "Really? I didn't know your father was in the army."

Caleb gritted his teeth but said nothing. I suspected the topic wasn't one he loved to talk about, but Cole didn't stop.

"And his mother was a flight attendant who…"

"Okay, Cole, let's stop talking about me," Caleb interrupted. "How do you like the stir-fry?"

It was weird that Caleb had deliberately changed the topic. Even Cole had been surprised, but he obeyed his friend. I noticed that Cole had used the past tense to talk about Caleb's parents' occupation. I wasn't sure if that indicated whether they were dead or whether they were no longer working.

After the meal, Caleb volunteered to see his friend off. They talked on the front porch for a while. As much as I wanted to stay out of Caleb's life, I wanted to know what he was keeping from me.

I snuck to the front window, straining my ears to hear what they were saying.

"…not fair, Caleb," Cole was saying. "Aren't you going to ever tell her about them?"

Caleb was silent for a while before he answered. "She doesn't have to know."

Why would he say that? Why would my fiancé think it wasn't necessary for me to know about his past? Just then, Caleb looked back as if he knew I had been listening. I sank to the floor almost immediately, my heart racing fast. Had he seen me? Without waiting to know, I crawled to the kitchen, feeling my hands tremble.

When Caleb returned, he found me cleaning the dishes. He didn't say anything as he crossed the room to me, planting a kiss on my forehead.

"I love you, Natalie," was all he said. "And I am going to change for good."

Day
64
Sixty-Four

His promise that things would change lasted for exactly three days and two hours.

"That's it," I said as I looked at the woman in our bed. "I am done. We're done. I thought that loving you was stronger than hating our problems, but it isn't. You promised me that things would change if I came back. You promised me, Caleb!"

I looked at the binder of wedding plans on our nightstand. To think that it was all going to go to waste made me want to tear my hair out. There was nothing that could be done anymore. We tried for two months to make our relationship work, and it was the same thing over and over again. Nothing was improving.

Instead, I was his punching bag. I was tired of being his punching bag. There was a time when I thought that leaving home and falling in love with another man was what I wanted. What would be best for me. I was wrong about that. If I was being honest with myself, we had jumped into things too fast. I loved him, but I couldn't keep doing this.

"What are you talking about?"

"I'm talking about us, Caleb. We can't keep doing this, and nothing is changing. Nothing at all. I thought that it would, and I thought that things would get better. Maybe it's just because I'm young and dumb, but nothing is improving, and I don't know what else I can do to make it better."

"We can make this work."

"No, we can't. Your demons are eating you alive, and they are devouring this relationship. It's not healthy for either of us."

"I'll do anything, darling. Don't leave me. I need you like you need me. We're made for each other."

I paused for a moment. They were the same words that I had heard countless times before, but still, I hoped that something would change. He made me feel like an entirely different person. Being with Caleb was amazing when it was good. But it was also a nightmare when things were horrible.

"Will you go to therapy?"

"I will do anything you want as long as you keep making those wedding plans. Don't let me scare you off, babe."

After a moment, I nodded. "In the morning, we are going to get you an appointment with a therapist, and I will start trying to find a wedding dress."

"We can do this."

More than anything, I wanted it to be the truth.

The next morning, I called one of my friends at the college to ask if he knew any psychotherapists. The guy directed me to one who stayed close to Caleb's home. I figured that it wouldn't be stressful for him since he wouldn't have to walk far to the shrink's office.

Caleb didn't object when I told him about the therapist.

In fact, he was happy to start his sessions. After I booked him with the therapist, he was told to start the next day. I decided not to follow him so he wouldn't feel embarrassed. Instead, I focused on my work and how I would help him get a job as soon as possible.

The next day, I left for school after making Caleb's breakfast. I had re-enrolled after realizing my education was failing from just online classes alone.

I reminded him about his appointment, and he told me that he had not forgotten. I was immersed in pure delight as I left. My life was about to get meaningful. I was going to experience a love life with no constant ups and downs.

"What is this that's going around?" Lauren asked me as soon as we met up.

I frowned. "What do you mean?"

"People are saying that you're crazy."

I chuckled. "What?"

"You asked for the address of a psychiatrist."

I shook my head. "Psychotherapist."

"Same thing," Lauren grunted. "Why would you even do that? Who the hell did you ask?"

It was Abel Goodman. Apparently, he wasn't a *good man.* I had confided in him, and he had gone to tell others. What was wrong with people?

"It's for Caleb," I told my friend, not minding what people were saying.

Caleb's decision to meet a therapist was bigger than anything else. They weren't going to douse the fame of my excitement.

"Really? That monster wants to see a shrink?"

"Yes," I shrieked in happiness. "He's finally going to save himself and our relationship."

Lauren rolled her eyes. "Good for you, but I still don't trust him."

However, when I got home, Caleb was there, his gaze fixed on the football match showing on TV. I glanced at my watch, noting the time. His appointment should have started ten minutes ago. Why was he still in the house?

"Caleb?" I said to him. "Did you forget? Why are you still here?"

He didn't look at me. My fiancé appeared preoccupied with the game. Just watching him do that, I felt my heart breaking again.

"Caleb, you need to talk to me."

That was when he peeled his eyes off the screen and faced me. His expression was unreadable.

"I needed to see this game."

"But… but your appointment." My lips quavered. "You promised me."

Caleb rose to his feet, flexing his muscles. I took a step back, expecting him to hit me like he always had. But that wasn't what he did. Instead, he pulled me close to him, my head resting on his broad chest.

"Don't worry," he said, stroking my hair. "I'll go next time."

Forever Yours

Day
68
Sixty-Eight

The smell of beer and whiskey entered the room long before Caleb did. He didn't say a word as he stormed to the coffee table – a wooden one that wouldn't break the next time he threw me onto it – and grabbed the binder of wedding plans.

"What are you doing?" I asked as he started tearing pages out of the book.

"Burning these plans. I have decided that I will not be going to therapy, and you can't make me," he said, his words slurred as he tossed pages into the fireplace.

I watched with tears in my eyes as all of the plans that I had made burned to a crisp.

"You need therapy. We can go together and talk to the therapist."

"We don't need it. You are going to be with me until the end of time whether I go to therapy or not. There is no choice, Natalie."

He stared at me with a sinister smile as the blood in my veins turned to ice.

"What are you talking about, Caleb? Come on, I think the drinks have gone to your head, and we should get you into bed."

"No."

"Well, how about you sit on the couch with me, and we can watch a movie? Come on, babe, let's relax. This is nothing that can't be dealt with in the morning."

"I won't be going to therapy."

"Okay, Caleb. I love you either way. You know that. Now, come sit down, and let's watch a movie."

After a moment, the smile fell away, and he flopped onto the couch beside me. I ran my fingers through his hair as I searched through the movies until I was sure I had found something that would put him to sleep.

I waited two hours after the snoring had begun before I grabbed the phone and called Lauren. She showed up in under half an hour and helped load my suitcase into the back of her car.

"I told you he wasn't going to change," Lauren said to me after driving in silence for a long time.

I was staring out the window, unable to tell her that she had been right. Why had I deluded myself? Caleb was impossible to change. Why was I trying so hard to do that? The wind whipped my hair back as Lauren's car sped past buildings, heading toward a place where I could cry and not bother anyone. Caleb always complained about that. I couldn't even cry in peace. But I didn't dare to talk back to him. It would only trigger his rage. Love was indeed the captivity I had chosen.

"What are you going to do now?" Lauren continued.

There was nothing on my mind right now. Maybe a cup of coffee would do, but I didn't want to stress out Lauren. She had been through a lot because of me.

"Nothing," I lied, but my best friend could sense it.

"You know, you can always tell me anything," she reminded me.

"There's nothing to talk about, Lauren."

But my friend wasn't giving in. She soon slowed down the car, peering at the side view mirror to watch out for cars behind her. By the time I knew what she was doing, Lauren had turned the car around, heading toward the direction we were just coming from.

"What are you doing?" I asked, alarmed.

"Oh, don't worry, I'm not taking you back to that monster," she answered. "I saw a diner several miles back. On me."

I sighed. Despite my stomach rumbling, I protested. "I'm not hungry."

"You're not going to tell me that."

Lauren stopped at the diner for real. I didn't even complain as she pulled me inside and ordered our meals. As I ate in silence, grateful that my friend had not given up on me, my eyes caught the appearance of someone outside the diner. It was Cole Watkins! What was he doing here?

"Cole?"

Lauren, who had her food in her mouth, glared at me, wondering what I was talking about. I raced out of the diner and got to Cole before he could drive away. He was walking out of the designer shop close to the restaurant.

"Cole!" I called out.

The man was surprised to see me there. "Hey, Natalie. Great to see you again."

I flashed him a tired smile. "Same."

"What are you doing here?"

Before I could respond, Lauren's voice came from behind me. She had gotten to me, wiping her mouth with the back of her hand.

"She's with me. I'm her friend. Who the hell are you?"

"Lauren, this is Cole Watkins, Caleb's childhood friend."

Lauren's look of disbelief wasn't hard to see. "Caleb has a friend? How believable!"

I nudged her in the ribs. The last thing I wanted to happen was Cole suspecting that my relationship with Caleb wasn't rosy. I wanted to keep his abuse a secret. Only Lauren and my mother knew about it. If my father ever found out, he'd reign hell upon him.

"Cole, it was nice seeing you," I said. "We have to go back in now."

Caleb's friend smiled. "Bye, Natalie. You too, Lauren."

As we watched him drive off in his Ford, my best friend asked me what Cole did for a living. I told her that he was a guard at the Federal Prison.

"He looks rich for a prison guard," she noted. "Are we even sure that's what he does?"

I shook my head. "I believe whatever Caleb says. He can't lie to me."

Her look of disbelief glared as she heard my response. "Seriously, Natalie? The dude lies every single time. How are you still believing him?"

"His past life is his business, not mine."

"No one is saying it's your business," replied Lauren. "But I'm interested in knowing who Cole is. If you're not, I don't care. My cousin is a cop. I can always ask him to look into Cole."

We were now back inside the diner. I took my seat and stared at my food, wondering if I should eat or not. Something about what Lauren had said troubled me. Yes, Cole appeared affluent for a man who watched over convicts.

"What if your boyfriend is into something shady? Are you still going to say it's not your business? The cops may be after him. For all we know, he might be some mafia lord, or terrorist from another country."

"He is American."

"Doesn't mean anything, Natalie," Lauren insisted. "What does he *really* do for a living? How is he living in a place that big?"

It had never crossed my mind that Caleb could be doing something illicit. Lauren was right. Maybe he *was* a drug dealer. Cole could be an accomplice. I had never even thought about the possibility of Caleb using drugs. That could be the reason for his hot temper and irrational behavior. It must be why he didn't want to see a therapist.

However, there was nothing like that in his place to prove my suspicions. I mean, if Caleb consumed hard drugs, I would have seen traces of it. The only rebuttal for that would be that he hid them well. Caleb was smart, so that wasn't much of an argument.

Yet, I didn't want to accept what Lauren was saying. In fact, if Caleb *was* a dangerous man, it was more reason for her to stay out of my life. I didn't want him hurting her, too. This was my cross. I was going to bear it alone.

"No, Lauren," I said to her. "Don't go digging into Cole's past or Caleb's. Please."

Lauren grunted and started eating. "Whatever you say."

Day
70
Seventy

But Lauren didn't listen. She said she cared about me and wasn't going to let some man kill me before fighting back. Lauren called her cousin, who did a good job in finding out who Cole Watkins really was.

"I found him," she said to me as she walked into the room, scrolling through something on her phone.

I frowned. "What are you talking about?"

"I found Cole Watkins!"

I slammed the can of coke in my hand on the dresser beside me. How could she? I had warned her explicitly not to do that.

Lauren ignored me. "He isn't a prison guard."

That was enough to catch my attention. I hurried to her side and stared at the information on her phone. She was right. Cole Watkins wasn't a guard. He was a psychiatrist!

"He works at the Federal Mental Facility," Lauren read out. "At least, they are both right about him working for the government."

I walked back to the bed and fell on it, gazing at the ceiling and realizing I was wrong again. Caleb *had* lied to me. He didn't seem to have *any* truth coming out of him. Why didn't Caleb disappoint for once?

"That's not all," Lauren continued, now sitting beside me. "I tried to look into Caleb, too."

I raised my head to look at her. "Oh, no."

"My cousin couldn't get anything on him, other than that he worked as a teacher in an elementary school several years ago, and you won't believe this, he is the son of a senator."

That explained his money. Caleb was the son of a rich man. However, Cole had talked about Caleb's father being a soldier and his mother being a flight attendant. Had his childhood friend lied about that, too?

"Okay, this makes sense," Lauren went on. "His father worked for the army before he quit and became a politician. Two years ago, he went missing and hasn't been found to this very day. His mother died twenty years ago in a plane crash caused by terrorists."

I felt my heart sink. Caleb's story was very sad. Anyone with that sort of past would definitely act like him. The dude was broken.

"That's all there is," my best friend concluded. "Nothing about him having been married or his wife dying. He may have been right about his parents, but it doesn't explain anything. It doesn't explain why he lied about Cole's occupation."

"There was a reason I told you not to dig into their past," I said to Lauren. "Caleb doesn't like to talk about what happened to him. He isn't going to be happy that I know about this."

"Are you going to tell him that you do?"

I shook my head. "No."

"Great," Lauren said and stood up from the bed. We have one more thing to do, though. Cole's workplace isn't far from here. If you're not prepared to walk into his office and ask him questions about Caleb, I am."

When I looked at her, I knew she meant it.

Cole Watkins' office was on the third floor of the government psychiatric hospital. When we got to the waiting room, a male nurse attended to us. I didn't know if he thought we were crazy by the way he seemed to eye us.

"How may I help you?" he asked.

Lauren flashed him a smile. "We are looking for Cole Watkins. Dr. Cole Watkins."

"And you are?"

"Elena Porter and Rachel Scott."

I glared at Lauren. She never told me that we would be lying about our names. When I caught the nurse staring at me, I broke into a friendly grin.

"Alright," the nurse said. "I'll inform him."

"What was that about?" I whispered to Lauren. "Elena Porter and Rachel Scott?"

Lauren facepalmed herself. She appeared frustrated that I wasn't understanding the plan. It wasn't my fault. The girl hadn't told me everything I needed to know.

"Natalie, if we had told the nurse our real names, and he had gone ahead to tell Cole, do you really think he would let us into his office? He is keeping Caleb's secret. To discover the truth, we need to lie."

What she said made perfect sense to me. I had strong doubts that Cole would be pleased to see us. We weren't even supposed to know what he truly did for a living. The nurse soon arrived, wearing a polite smile.

"Dr. Watkins is in his office," he told us. "You can go in now."

Cole's office was posh and comfortable for a doctor of the mentally insane. The man, himself, had his back turned to us when we entered, reading a magazine that appeared interesting to him.

When he spun around in his office chair to greet us, the shock that came over him was impossible to miss. Cole quickly rose to his feet, looking like he had just seen a ghost.

"Natalie," he stammered. "La…"

"Lauren," my best friend chipped in. "But you are one hell of a pretender, Dr. Watkins. Just like how you lied to my friend that you're a prison guard."

"I had to," came Cole's reply.

"Why? Did he threaten to kill you?"

I stopped Lauren before she could go any further. Her questions were rattling Cole, and I didn't want him to feel that way. Without waiting for him to offer me a seat, I took one, placing my handbag gently on his desk. Lauren did the same, refusing to stop grinning.

"Dr. Watkins, you can sit," I said in a calm tone. "We're not here to scare you. We only came to ask you some questions."

But Cole didn't take his seat. He remained standing, staring down at us. His scared look soon vanished, replaced by one that seemed to jab at my heart.

"How did you find me?" he asked.

"You're not so hard to find, Dr. Cole Jeremy Watkins."

Yeah, Lauren's cousin had been able to provide us with everything about Cole, down to his favorite meal. It was only Caleb we couldn't find much about, and I found that unsettling. It was almost as though someone had cleared out most of his records.

"You need to leave," Cole said.

"And why would we do that?" Lauren's tone was now very unfriendly. "You know something about Caleb. Who is he, really?"

Cole kept a straight face. "I can't really answer that. Natalie, Lauren, as much as I would love to help you, it's not my job to tell you about Caleb."

Lauren wasn't going to buy that. "So, whose job is it? Do we have to talk to someone? Dr. Watkins, why did you lie to my best friend?"

I placed a hand on Lauren's. It was time for her to stop talking. If I allowed my friend to go on, she would end up insulting Cole and ruining everything. I was now very interested in knowing who Caleb was.

"Cole," I called him by his first name. "You need to tell me something. I don't know a single thing about Caleb, and you seem to. I heard you that day. There is something he should have told me, but my fiancé doesn't think it's any of my business. Whatever it is, I think I deserve to know."

Dr. Watkins took his seat. "You don't, Natalie. Caleb likes to keep his private life, *private*. He wants to protect you."

I raised an eyebrow in question. "From what?"

"That I can't tell you. I'm sorry."

That was when Lauren lost it. She shot up from her chair, slamming both hands on the desk. "You're going to tell us, dude, or I am going to force it out of you."

"Hey, Lauren. Stop, please." That was me begging.

"Restrain your friend, Natalie," Cole growled. "Or I am going to call security."

Lauren appeared to calm down when she heard this. She backed away from the desk, picking up my bag.

"Let's get out of here, Nat."

As I turned to follow her, my eyes fell on a book on Cole's table. It had the name "Patients' Information" written on it. That was when I remembered the doctor-patient confidentiality that made doctors keep information about their patients to themselves. Was Cole not saying anything because

Caleb was his patient? But that would be impossible. If Caleb had been a patient of this facility, it would have shown on his record.

"Dr. Watkins," I said. "Did Caleb ever come here as a patient?"

Cole stared at me for a few seconds before he shook his head and replied, "I can't tell you anything about Mr. McCord, other than that we were childhood friends. I'm sorry that I lied to you about my job, but Caleb wanted me to. He was trying to prevent this. As I said earlier, that man is only out to protect you. He is a good person."

Maybe I believed him.

Day
76
Seventy-Six

Lauren was gone when the front door to her home was kicked in. Maybe it was a blessing that she hadn't been home. If she had been, I wasn't sure that Caleb would have left her alive. Even as he grabbed me and wrestled me out to the car, he had a crazed look in his eyes. I screamed, hoping that one of the neighbors would hear me, but there wasn't a single person who bothered to even look out their window. I was tossed in the trunk of his car, plunged into darkness the second he closed it.

I don't know how long he drove for, but I felt it when the road became bumpy. My body was tossed around in the trunk while everything else he had in there slammed into me. Groaning, I curled into a ball and hoped that it would be over soon. My heart was hammering in my chest, but there was a part of me that felt sad for him. What had happened in the days since I left that pushed him this far? What demons were he facing?

I wanted to help him and help myself. There was a part of me that wanted to hate him, but the part of me that wanted to love him was greater.

Finally, the car stopped, and the trunk opened. Caleb grinned, cigarette caught between his lips, and a thin trail of smoke wafted toward the stars. He grabbed my bicep, his fingers digging deep, and he hauled me out of the trunk and to my feet.

"Walk," he said, shoving my shoulder. "Get your ass in the cabin."

"No."

He chuckled; his breath was hot on the back of my neck as he leaned down.

"Get your ass inside the damn cabin before I make you," he whispered.

There was something about the whisper and the tension in the air that had me nearly running for the cabin. He was close behind me, his steps nearly falling on the back of my heels. Once I crossed the threshold, he pulled the door shut behind him. I could hear the key turning in the lock.

I waited for a few minutes before running my hands along the door, desperately trying to find the deadbolt. My heart was hammering in my chest, and I could hear the blood rushing in my ears. The world around me was spinning, and the walls were closing in.

There was no lock on this side of the door.

Pounding my fists against it, I screamed until my voice was hoarse. I ran around, checking all of the windows, only to find them boarded up. There was nothing I could do. I was trapped. Caleb had captured me, and he had locked me away from the world. There was no help coming for me.

"Well, it looks like it's finally time that you and I have that talk that we keep dancing around about," Caleb said, his voice startling me awake.

I blinked and backed away from him, but there was nowhere I could go. The cabin was a single room with a bathroom attached. There would be no hiding and no escape. I was at his mercy. I only hoped that the man who was before me was the same man who still loved me. It was the only chance I had at making it out, of whatever this was, alive.

The thought chilled me to my core. Coming to terms with the fact that the person I loved the most would likely be the one to kill me was not an easy thought to bear. I stared at him, my eyes wide, and my pulse racing. He took a swig of amber liquid from the bottle in his hand before tossing it to the side.

"You think that you can just leave me like that? What happened to us being in this together? What happened to loving each other and starting a life together? You are my everything, Natalie. I thought that I meant the same thing to you too, but I guess not. You keep hurting me at every single turn. You know that you aren't that great, right? I could have any woman that I want. But no, I chose you. The loser with a love of hiking."

I gasped and backed away from him as he advanced. "I thought that you loved me."

"I do love you, babe. So much it hurts. I just wish that you loved me that much, too. But no. Things get hard, and you keep leaving me. What happened to working through things together, Natalie? What happened to that? Were you just lying to me to escape your shitty life?"

"No!" Tears streamed down my face. "I love you, Caleb. But you keep hurting me. I want to help you. I would do everything that I can to help you."

"Well, clearly, that is a lie. You don't love me like I love you. You wanted to leave me. That just isn't going to happen."

He lunged. It was too quick to escape, but I tried. His fingers grazed my neck before latching onto my hair. With a yelp, I was dragged backwards and tossed against the stone fireplace. There was a heavy thud as I fell to the floor, and blood matted my hair to my head. I crawled away from him but not fast enough. His hand wrapped around my ankle, squeezing tight as he pulled me back. Once he was above me, his fist collided with my face. I heard a sickening crunch as my nose broke, and blood poured down my face.

"Stop!" I screamed as I tried to bat his hands away while he grabbed at me. "Caleb! Stop! This isn't you. Please."

He laughed, the sound echoing through the tiny cabin. "Oh, love, this is *exactly* who I am when you try to leave me. How could you do that to me? We were supposed to be together until the end, but you tried to stop that from happening. You tried to tear us apart."

"I would never! I just wanted to get us some help, Caleb. I thought that leaving for a few days would give us both some time to think!"

"Liar!"

His fist rammed into my side. Another crunch. I gasped for air, holding onto my side as I tried to curl up. Before I could, the toe of his work boot cracked against my back. My screams filled the cabin as tears and blood ran like rivers down my face.

"No!"

"Yes! You are! You tried to leave me! You wanted to get away from me, and you wanted nothing to do with me. I thought that you were going to be the love of my life, but you're not. You're just like my wife."

His wife? Was he still lying about that? Who really was this insane man?

"Caleb," I said slowly.

He grinned and raised an eyebrow. "Yes, love?"

"What did you do to your wife?"

"Don't worry about that," he said as he walked to the door. "You just worry about what's going to happen if you try to leave me again."

He paused at the door before turning around. Crouching, he grabbed my ankle and twisted. I screamed as the bone broke.

"What the hell?!"

"Now, you won't leave me again," Caleb said with a chuckle. "If I have to break it every time your ankle heals, I will. Don't push me."

"Please, take me to the hospital. I love you, remember? And you love me."

"I know I love you," he said.

"Just stop hurting me, please."

He grunted and let go of my ankle. I wondered if I should tell him about my visit to Cole. If I did, then Caleb would probably put two and two together. He would know that I had found out about his past and the fact that he was never married. I didn't want that. I was in enough pain already.

"You went to Cole," Caleb said and grinned more as he saw my reaction of surprise.

"I...I..." I began to stutter.

The slap that shut me up was one I had not expected. I cried as my vision spun, my cheek stinging like it had been set on fire. Caleb moved away from me...for now. I could hear him wheezing in rage.

"Don't you dare lie to me!" he said. "I know that you and Lauren went to Cole's office. You have been investigating me. You know how I don't like to talk about myself."

"It wasn't my fault," I managed to say.

"Bullshit! You were snooping around."

"I'm sorry!"

"No, you're not. What do you really want to know about me? That my mom died, and my father is still missing? What exactly would you like to know, Natalie? Tell me. I'm going to answer your questions."

It seemed like a trick. Caleb was telling me that I could now ask him questions and get answers. Would his answers come as punches or words?

"I hate people ignoring me, Natalie!" he yelled. "What the fuck do you want to know?"

I pressed a palm against my cheek, flinching from the pain. Around Caleb, it was impossible to act right. If I decided to keep quiet and ask him nothing, he could get pissed off and start hurting me again.

"Your wife," I started. "There's no record of you being married."

Caleb shook his head. "So, you dug that deep?"

I dared not to look at him. "Lauren made me do it."

"That friend of yours is going to ruin your life, and it's so sad how you keep running back to her. You should be running to me, Natalie. I am the only one who can save you."

I held back my tears. It would be another problem weeping in front of him. Caleb took his seat on the floor, staring at his fingers. This I knew because I was now looking at him. He seemed very calm; the sort of man who would not dare to hurt a woman or break her ankle. I didn't know which one hurt me the most – my ankle or my cheek.

"I had a wife, Natalie," Caleb answered. "But you would never find any record of her. She isn't part of my life anymore. There is no need to know about her."

It scared me the way he said that. Caleb had wiped out her existence. Would he do that to me, too? Would he make it appear as though I had never been in his life and move to another woman? What exactly had happened to his former wife?

"She didn't die?"

Caleb rose to his feet after I asked that.

"*She* is not important, Natalie. You don't have to worry about her. She isn't coming to destroy what we have."

That wasn't why I asked. However, Caleb was thinking of something else. He thought I was bothered that his ex-wife would steal him from me. I wasn't even sure if she was still alive or not.

"You'll wait for me, right?" Caleb begged with his eyes.

I had no choice but to nod. He smiled and walked toward the door.

"At least, let me out of here."

Caleb just left without saying anything. I listened to the key turn in the lock before I succumbed to the pain.

Day
78
Seventy-Eight

Caleb hadn't visited the cabin in two days. Two days, where I had been in and out of consciousness, the pain too overwhelming to bear at times. It was only a few hours earlier that I found a bottle of oxy in his medicine cabinet. After taking one, the pain seemed to melt away. I had dragged myself across the floor to the kitchen and made a makeshift splint for my ankle. Mandatory first-aid programs for school had finally come in handy.

I looked at my ankle with a bitter laugh. There didn't seem to be a way out of here. I was going to be tied to Caleb for the rest of his life. Manic episodes and all. Maybe one day, I would be able to get him help. When he was stable, he was a loving man. He was soft and gentle, willing to admit that he needed help. When he went into monster mode, I didn't know how many of my bones would end up broken that night. There had to be a better way to live.

The door opened, and Caleb walked in with a large bottle of water at his side.

"Hello, love. How are you doing today?"

"Fine," I said through gritted teeth.

"Try not to sound too excited to see me," he said as he looked around the room and spotted the pill bottle on the little table beside me. "I see that you found your medicine. I brought you some water since the cabin doesn't have anything hooked up for the season yet."

"Thank you," I whispered, knowing that it was the answer he wanted.

Tears burned my eyes. How could someone I loved do this to me?

He held the bottle to my lips after unscrewing the top. I let the cool water wash down my throat, desperate for the hydration. When I finished, he pulled the bottle away and put the top back on before sitting beside me on the couch.

"I think that there are some things I need to get off my chest," Caleb said as he set the bottle on the coffee table and slung one arm over the back of the couch. His gaze traveled to the blood stain on the floor before looking back at me. "I'm sorry about all of this, my love. If there was any other way to make you see things my way, I would, but you just don't understand what you mean to me. How special you are. I really don't want to have to keep hurting you like this. I'm sure that you don't want me to hurt you, either

"No," I said, my voice barely more than a whisper. "What do you want to talk about, babe?"

The term of endearment sent a pang through my heart. I loved him. After everything that he had done to me, to us, I still loved him more than I was willing to admit. Although, if it was going to get me out of this cabin alive, I would shower him with all the love he wanted.

"We need to talk about the knife that you keep stabbing me in the back with," Caleb said as he twisted a strand of my hair around his finger. "You see, I know that I am not the easiest man to love, but I thought that we could overcome all of that. I thought that our relationship was more important to you than my demons. However, you keep proving me wrong."

"Loving you is more important than how you deal with your demons."

"See, I almost believed you that time, but you have been saying the same thing for weeks. You keep saying that you love me, but I don't believe it anymore. How do you keep doing this to somebody you love?"

"I *do* love you, Caleb. I love you so much."

"That's just not good enough anymore, Natalie. You and I are going to be together forever, one way or another. I'm not going to lose you again. Although, it would help if you stopped acting like a child and started acting like the woman I fell in love with."

"I *am* the woman that you fell in love with."

His hand fisted in my hair, yanking my head back sharply.

"No. You aren't. Now, I am going to suggest that you stop lying to me."

"I'm not lying to you," I whispered. "I wouldn't lie to you, babe. I love you so much. We can work through all of this together. We can still get married, have kids, and grow old together. I want all of those things with you. You know that I do. I want to be the person at your side for the rest of your life. I want all of that. Every part of it. You and me, forever."

"You're lying to me again. I don't like it when you lie to me. You know that."

"I'm not lying."

"Yes, you are. I won't punish you for it this time. Instead, I am going to go for a walk. Maybe go into town and get some food. When I get back, you and I will talk about all of the things that are going to be in store for our future."

He let go of my hair and got off the couch. I watched as he walked to the door and left once more. It was only after he was gone that the tears started falling.

He lied. When Caleb came back, he tried to drown me. I really had no idea why he was that cruel to me. I couldn't resist as he dragged me to the bathtub in the cabin, already filled with water, and plunged my head into it.

I have had two major near death-by-drowning experiences. I won't go into details of the unfortunate incidents, but I would tell you the things that I had not thought of. The physical environment. The water. The toll the struggle had taken on my body.

In each case, I had not been in a place where other human beings were; therefore, the possibility that I could be saved did not exist at the moment. My eyes had just searched the area, frantically looking for someone to rescue me. The first time, I had forgotten to even yell for help because my brain had been in a shock mode. I had been pulled out unconsciously after someone saw me at the last moment and jumped in to my rescue. The second time, however, I had remembered to scream at the top of my lungs for help, but not until I had resurfaced from the water. Thankfully, someone heard me.

Having almost drowned twice in my past, I now lived with a sinister phobia for water.

But it didn't matter to Caleb. He knew my fear, and he was using it to torture me.

Maybe that was why, when my body crashed into the cold bath water this time, my life hadn't just flashed before my very eyes. Instead, it had projected forward. My brain got transported into a world of certain death. Maybe they were just some near-death experiences, but as I struggled to raise my head from the water, I pictured the police notifying my mother about her only daughter's tragic death in a cabin, and that was if Caleb was nice enough to leave my body there. I thought about my father, who would show no remorse and, possibly, blame me for dying. Lauren would cry; I was sure of it. She would tell everyone it was Caleb, but there might be no evidence left.

Caleb pulled me out seconds later, chuckling at the sight of me gasping for air.

"See," he said. "This is what happens when you try to play tough."

I had never tried to play tough with him. My intention was to find out more about him. How was that a crime? Why was he making me pay for it? I wished Lauren was here to see this. She had put me in trouble and now, I was paying for it with my lungs.

"Let's go again," Caleb's voice came, and before I could react to that, the water came for my face again.

It was quite simple. I was going to die. There would be no one to save me. I would drown in Caleb's hands. He would kill me and be satisfied that he did.

The water rushed into my lungs, filling me as I continued to fight. It was surprising how the water made me feel like I was on fire, like my lungs would burst open any second. It was the need for air, the need to grasp for something that would save my life. The dark overpowered me, the silence adding to my dread. Who would notice if I was gone? Who would save me from this death?

The darkness was stronger now. I gave into it, and there was complete silence…

"Natalie?" A voice was pulling me out of the dark.

When I opened my eyes, Caleb was bending over me, his eyes watery as he stared at me. I didn't know what had happened. I had no idea why I was on the floor, shivering and wet as though I had gone for a bath in the sea.

That wasn't true. I had never been to the sea and would never dream of doing so. However, I had gotten my face shoved in a bathtub and almost died. This was done by the man who was now crying in front of me.

"Natalie," he said, his voice almost breaking. "You're awake!"

I tried to sit up, but I couldn't. My body still trembled, and there was a numbing pain in my waist and neck. For someone who just had water rushing into their lungs, I felt thirsty, which was weird. My parched throat itched at the same time.

"Caleb," I called his name, which he responded to by slipping his hands into mine. "What happened?"

"It's all my fault," Caleb answered, now crying. "I made a mistake. I am so sorry."

"You…you tried to kill me," I said to him.

"That was wrong of me," Caleb said. "It's never going to happen again."

I didn't know what to say. When Caleb had tried to kill me, the look in his eyes was demonic. It was like he had been taken over by the devil Pastor

Cooper had talked about. Now that he realized what he had done, Caleb was remorseful, weeping like an innocent child.

It would suddenly make sense if Cole had said he was a patient at the facility. That had to be the only explanation for this insane behavior. I tried to move away from him, but even if I did, Caleb had already instilled enough fear in me.

"Come on," he said. "Let me help you up."

"Was that what you did to your wife?" I heard myself asking.

Caleb didn't answer. Instead, he carried me to a bed in the room and put me down on it. After he watched me for a while, he began to stroke my hair.

"You'll be fine," said Caleb.

"I need an answer, Caleb. Was that what you did to your wife?"

"I said, I don't want to talk about her," he answered, wiping the tears on his face. "We can't keep talking about her."

"I just need to know if you're capable of murdering someone."

Caleb stopped touching my hair. He folded his arms and exhaled loud enough for me to hear.

"Her name was Mandy," Caleb said. "I loved her like I love you. We got married when we turned eighteen. Mandy was ready to spend the rest of her life with me. I was prepared to do that, too."

I waited for him to continue. As slow as his confessions might be, I wanted to hear everything. Even if it meant losing a limb or getting drowned, I was determined to hear Caleb's full story.

"Then she just changed. Mandy stopped loving me. It hurt me. She had promised to be my wife forever, and suddenly, she was backing out. I wasn't going to have that, so I made her disappear. It was better if I couldn't see her again. That way, I would stop feeling enraged at everyone and everything."

"How did you make her disappear?" I asked.

It took Caleb a few seconds before he said, "My father made it happen. I called to tell him everything. He was angry, too. Then he came home one day and asked me to go on a vacation alone. When I got back, Mandy was gone. That was the last time I ever heard from her."

It made perfect sense now. Caleb's father was a rich man. He had the money to make anyone vanish from the face of the Earth. If Mandy had hurt Caleb, then he would have certainly taken her out of his life.

Yet, I didn't want to believe Mandy was the one who hurt Caleb. It was possible that he beat her too, or acted like a psychiatric patient around her. Mandy might have seen what a horrible person he was and given up. That's why Caleb didn't want me to give up. If I did, he would have to kill me himself, considering his father was nowhere to be found, and he wouldn't be around to make me disappear. I wanted to ask him about the man but decided to defer it. There would always be time for that question.

"I don't want you to leave me, Natalie," Caleb was saying, holding my hands again. "If you do, I'm scared of what I would have to do."

Yeah, I figured that much. It scared me that I was left with no choice. Leaving Caleb was suicide itself. If I stayed with him, I wouldn't last long, either.

"I don't want to leave you, Caleb," I said to him. "But this pain you keep inflicting upon me, I can't take it anymore."

I was crying now. Caleb wiped my tears with his thumb. If I didn't remember what he did to me in the bathtub, I would have thought he was actually caring.

"It's not going to happen again. Trust me."

As always, he lied. By the time it was dark, Caleb's madness was back. He barged into the room, breathing heavily in rage.

"You bitch! I shouldn't have told you about Mandy. Now, you have to go back into that other room!"

"Caleb, stop!" I cried as he pulled me from the bed, dragging me all the way to the room where he had first locked me in.

"I should have kept it a secret, but you made me tell you!" Caleb continued, finally bringing me into the room.

I cried when he let go of me. Caleb glared at me as he stood in the doorway.

"Natalie Grace, stay the hell out of my life! I hate you!"

With that, he slammed the door and walked away. Only the silence surrounded me. I was totally helpless.

Day
80
Eighty

nother two days had passed, and there was still no sign of Caleb. The water bottle had run dry hours ago, and the pain in my body was numb from the oxy. If there was any time to escape, it would be tonight. Friday nights were his weakness. They always had been. He would get so drunk that he didn't know where he was. It was then that I would make my escape. When he was passed out, dead to the world, I would take off. How I was going to get the door open, I didn't know, but somehow, I would manage. All I had to do was wait.

Sure enough, he showed up late that night, stumbling and slurring his words. He was beyond plastered, and once he hit the mattress, he was fast asleep. I counted the minutes after his snores started, waiting until an hour had passed before I limped my way to the front door. His coat was hanging on a hook beside it. Quietly, I dug through his pockets until I found the keys to his car. Grinning, I pressed against the door. It opened right away.

Thank you, drunken Caleb, for forgetting to lock the door.

When I was outside, I locked the door. It would not keep him in there for long once monster Caleb appeared, but it would be long enough.

Limping and gritting my teeth against the pain, I made my way to the car. The moment I was in, and the car was running, I pressed my foot against the gas and turned the lights on. The car sped down the bumpy forest road, flying over the bumps and branches.

Once I made it to the main road, I stepped on the gas harder. The car roared as I drove around the curves. There had to be a hospital or a police station somewhere nearby.

The sun was rising by the time I pulled into the emergency lot of the hospital. The oxy had worn off over an hour ago, and the pain was radiating all through my body. Tears were streaming down my face as I stopped the car and fell out of the driver's door and onto the ground.

My world went black as I heard a nurse scream.

Day
83
Eighty-Three

The hospital room was pristine white, and the nurses were friendly, though there was one who kept urging me to speak with the police. I couldn't do it, though. No matter how much Caleb had hurt me, I still loved him. If I told the police everything that he had done, and everything I suspected that he had done to his wife, they would lock him up. He was troubled and disturbed. Caleb needed therapy, not prison.

It was after midnight when the phone in my room started ringing. I glanced at it, my heart racing in my chest as I reached for the receiver.

"Hello?"

There was heavy breathing on the other end of the line. My pulse sped up, the machines I was connected to screaming. For a few moments, nothing was said. Maybe it was someone who had dialed the wrong room. I was about to hang up when I heard words that made my heart stop.

"You didn't think escaping me would be so easy, did you?"

"Caleb," I called his name. "Why do you keep doing this to me?"

"It doesn't matter, Natalie," he said. "Just come home."

Unable to hold my tears, I slammed the phone down and prayed he wouldn't call again. There were a lot of things I wanted to tell Caleb, but my love for him restrained me. I didn't understand why I could love him so much after everything he had done to me. Maybe *I* was the one who was disturbed.

"Natalie?" a voice called my name.

I quickly wiped my tears and looked up to find Cole Watkins in my ward, a bunch of flowers in his hand. My first thought was to yell at him and send him out of my room. He had told Caleb about my visit to his office. If he had kept his mouth shut, I wouldn't have been in this mess.

However, I couldn't find the strength to do that. Seeing his sympathetic smile forced the tears out of me again. I buried my face in my palms, heaving as my body trembled. Cole came to my side, placing a hand on the small of my back.

"Natalie," he said. "It's okay. You need to recover."

"He did this to me," I confessed to the man.

But if he was surprised, he didn't act like it. Cole set down the flowers on my lap.

"I stopped by to see you."

When I raised my head to look at him, my misty eyes prevented me from seeing him clearly, coupled with a throbbing ache in my head.

"You knew about this? You knew what he did to me?"

Cole sighed. "I am only going to tell you that my friend is a troubled man. You have to end this. Don't go back to him. I'll leave now."

I grabbed his wrist before he could move away from me.

"Please, Cole, tell me everything."

I could see the sad look that spread across his face. Cole wanted to tell me, but something was stopping him from doing so.

I was right because he said, "I can't do that. The only way you can save yourself is not to go back to him. If you do, you're only going to hurt yourself more. Caleb is a helpless man. You can't save him."

Day
87
Eighty-Seven

"Hello, Natalie. I told you that escaping me, our love, wouldn't be that easy. It ends when one of us dies. Of course, this could be a long time from now. What I don't understand is why you keep leaving me. I thought that you loved me, Natalie. I love you, darling. So much. So very much. Like crazy. Please tell me that you love me."

I sighed and looked at my cell phone. Lauren had picked me up from the hospital yesterday, and she would have my head if she knew who I was talking to. Looking into the room, Lauren frowned and pointed at the phone.

"Mom," I said softly.

Lauren nodded and disappeared again.

"You wouldn't be lying to that annoying friend of yours, would you?"

"What does it matter?"

"It does matter. I thought that I could make you love me, Natalie. I did everything that I could to make sure that you would love me, but instead, you betrayed me. You broke my heart. Maybe part of it was my fault. I came on too strong. I don't understand how I lost the love of my life, but I will not live without you for another day."

"Caleb," I said, my voice becoming high-pitched as my heart beat faster. "What are you talking about?"

"Goodbye, Natalie, I love you."

It took ten minutes to convince Lauren to drive me to Caleb's house. She agreed only after she had called the police and told them that she had reason to believe a man was going to kill himself. I knew she was right. I knew the police needed to be contacted.

Knowing all of that didn't make walking into the bedroom we once shared any easier. Everything was as I had left them, as if he hadn't been in here since I left. With a racing pulse, I looked around the room. That was when I saw it.

The closet door was opened, and a rope was hanging over it, tied to the doorknob. Time seemed to come to a standstill as I walked forward. Tears welled in my eyes. It couldn't be him. It would never be him. Caleb would never do that to himself. He wouldn't do that to me. We loved each other. We were going to be together forever.

"Caleb?" I said as I opened the door. The breath was stolen from my lungs as I saw him hanging limply by his neck. "Babe, no. Caleb. Caleb. Wake up. This isn't funny anymore. I'm back, babe. We can be together now. Wake up. Wake up. Please, wake up."

Arms wrapped around my waist as I tried to get Caleb loose. Lauren pulled, trying to get me to let go and walk away. Still, I fought to get to him. This was all my fault. If I had been more understanding, loved him a little more, put more effort into our relationship, he would still be here.

"Come on," Lauren said softly. "The police will be here soon, and he's gone."

"No."

"Yes," Lauren said softly. She held me when I started to shake. It was my fault. "Let's go downstairs, and wait for the police."

No amount of wishing and hoping would bring him back. I looked at Caleb one more time, tears streaming down my face.

"I'll always love you," I whispered as I allowed Lauren to lead me away.

Caleb was gone, but it was true. I *would* always love him.

Day
88
Eighty-Eight

It was daytime by the time I walked into the hospital.

My legs grew heavy with every step I took, as though warning me not to complete this trip to the ward upstairs, where I knew he was waiting for me. But at the same time, I felt delighted by what I had heard over the phone an hour ago.

Caleb McCord was still alive. Somehow, he had survived his attempt to kill himself. I wouldn't have to cry over the fact that I had killed him.

I knew how Lauren would react if she heard I was going to visit him. But what choice did I really have? Caleb had chosen to hurt himself because of me.

That was enough to make me go running back to him, seeking his forgiveness.

"Miss Grace, right?" A nurse approached me, hugging a clipboard to her chest.

She appeared young and wore a beautiful smile, reminding me of the days when I was also like her. Those days had been the best of my life.

Even my relationship with Josh hadn't been ridden with so much pain. On days that my parents acted like shit, I could go to Josh and not worry about facing the same thing.

But I had not loved him the way I loved Caleb.

"Yes, that's me," I responded quickly, masking my sadness with a polite beam.

"You called in the morning," the nurse informed me. "The doctor thought it was best if Mr. McCord doesn't see anyone. At first, he didn't talk to anybody. But then, he started saying your name, and we had to call you back."

Really? That was what had happened? After calling the hospital to know if I could speak to Caleb, I had dozed off on the couch, only to be awoken by the hospital calling me. The hospital worker had simply said I could see Caleb.

"Can I see him now?"

"Sure," the nurse answered and led me to Caleb's ward.

Caleb was sitting in bed, massaging his left wrist and staring at nothing. When he saw me, his reaction was stuck between shock and excitement. His dark eyes glistened with tears, which broke my heart even more.

"Natalie," he said softly.

I didn't know what to think or say. The man in front of me was different from the one who had hurt me, hit me with his bare hands. I was looking at Caleb again, the real Caleb, like that first date at Whitman State Park.

"Caleb," I responded, hurrying to his side.

He held my hands, cradling them gently like I meant everything to him. I could still see the marks on his neck, where he had fastened the rope and tried to take his own life.

"You came? Thank you. I didn't know how to get to you. I couldn't bring myself to."

Hearing him say that softened my heart. It was ironic how I had just saved myself from him, escaping that cabin where he had locked me in for days and vowing that I would never go back to him. Yet, here I was, listening to his apologetic tones and remembering why I had fallen in love with him in the first place.

Caleb needed help. Maybe he was a broken man praying for a hand to pull him out of the pond of despair. Maybe he was battling demons known only to him, hoping for true redemption in his dark hell.

"Hey, I'm here," I told him, rubbing the back of his hands. "You're going to be fine."

"I'm sorry for everything, Natalie," Caleb said again.

"You don't have to apologize."

He was staring at me as he trembled, a man on the verge of tears. Caleb should apologize to me. To be honest, it was the only thing I needed him to do. For every time he had hurt me and broke my heart, for every night he slept with a woman that wasn't me, Caleb was supposed to ask for my forgiveness, to say sorry a billion times.

However, his weakness robbed me of that right. I didn't even see my pain, only his. The fact that I could have lost him sent a chill through me. No apology should come from him. I didn't need to hear his pleas. I needed him to stay alive.

"I have to tell you how sorry I am," he insisted. "This isn't your fault. It's mine."

"If I hadn't left you, you wouldn't have tried to kill yourself."

Caleb took his hands away from mine, withdrawing in shame. Something had crossed his mind, and he wasn't happy about it.

"Caleb?"

"I'm a bad person," he started. "A really bad person."

"No, you're not."

If Caleb was returning to his depressive state, it wasn't a good thing. He could leave this hospital and try to kill himself again.

"I shouldn't have hurt you just because I was broken."

I frowned at him, confused by his statement. "What do you mean by broken?"

"My childhood," Caleb answered, his tone wavering. "I grew up…"

I waited for him to explain. His shoulders dropped, burdened by an invisible weight of anguish.

"I really don't want to talk about it," he concluded.

I nodded, not planning to pressure him. Caleb had a past that he was hiding from me. I believed that looking into his past life would grant me knowledge about his triggers. Maybe if I could see his true identity, it would be a justification for his actions.

"You need to rest," I said, slowly rising to my feet.

As soon as I did that, Caleb grabbed my hand again. I jerked in fright, expecting him to hurt me. His grip was firm, exactly like the way he held me while raining punches on me. I didn't know why he was planning to beat me in the hospital ward with the nurses and doctors around.

After he saw my reaction, Caleb released his grip, lips trembling as he opened his mouth to say something.

"I'm sorry. I was trying to stop you from leaving."

Relief flooded me. Caleb wasn't trying to hit me. I was only panicking. The only thing I could do was nod. I wished he hadn't seen how scared I was. It wasn't my fault that I felt that way. Every move or gesture from Caleb reminded me of what he made me go through.

My phone began to ring in my pocket. I pulled it out and realized that Lauren was calling. It would be foolish to pick up the call in front of Caleb.

"I have to go," I said to him. "I'll be back, but take care of yourself."

When I left the ward, I picked up my best friend's call. She sounded so agitated when she came home, and I wasn't there.

"Where the hell are you?"

I stammered. "I went out for a walk."

Without being in her presence, I knew Lauren could see through my lie. Anyone could have guessed where I was, and they would have called me a fool.

"Don't bullshit me," Lauren answered. "You're meeting him again?"

"No, Lauren."

"Stop lying!"

I sighed. She was right. There was no point in trying to deceive her. Lauren knew I was too in love with Caleb to abandon him.

"I had to see him."

"You need help," came her response.

"He tried to kill himself!" I yelled at her, causing a nurse to shoot me a questioning look.

I seemed to have raised my voice.

"That's not your business."

"He was going to end his life because of me. How's that not my business? How could I have gotten over that?" My voice was barely a whisper.

"He hurt you, Natalie." Lauren wasn't giving in. "He's only messing with your mind, playing the victim card."

"The doctors had to revive him. He wasn't faking it."

I heard Lauren mutter some words over the phone that I couldn't make out. There was no doubt that she was frustrated. But how was she not seeing that it would have been my fault if Caleb died?

"That dude of yours is losing a bolt in his head. He's sick, and you need to leave him."

I was now outside the hospital, heading for my truck. A piece of paper was stuck between the windshield wipers, left there by someone who wanted me to see it.

"Please, Lauren," I said to my friend, removing the paper from my car and realizing it was just a flyer. "I just need to understand what's going on with him."

"I'm going to hate you for the rest of my life if anything happens to you."

The flyer was for a private therapist who lived close to my place. "Buckley's Mental Help" was the name on it. I didn't know if this was fate's way of agreeing to what Lauren had said.

"I'll call you later."

Lauren didn't say anything and cut the call. Her rage was expected. She was just looking out for me.

But I wasn't a kid. I knew what was best for me and what wasn't. Caleb McCord was broken. I vowed to fix him.

Yet, as I stared at the flyer in my hand, I thought about what Lauren had said. Maybe I should seek therapy. My best friend wasn't insinuating that I was insane. Neither did I see myself in that light. What harm could come from lying on a stranger's cushion and asking them about my own sanity?

As I got into the truck, I decided to put a call through to the center. A woman picked up after it rang only once, calmly speaking to me and asking for my details. She set up a session for me and told me that Buckley's Mental Help would send a car to pick me up on that particular day.

"Oh, great," I said to myself, cutting the call and staring at myself through the rear-view mirror. "I'm going to be seeing a shrink."

I didn't suppose that was a bad thing. The shrink could turn out to be good at his job. Caleb could use someone like him, too.

I tried to start the vehicle just as someone rapped on the window of my truck. For the second time, I was startled, shivering so much the key dropped from my hand and got lost somewhere under my car seat. But this time around, it wasn't from the fear of what Caleb did to me. A tall man was outside my truck, waving at me.

I rolled down the glass, wondering who he was and why he was trying to talk to me.

"Sorry to bother you, but are you Natalie Grace?"

I eyed him. "Who's asking?"

He reached for something in his pocket. When he brought his hand to my vision again, a police badge was gleaming in it.

"Detective Lawrence Powers," he answered. "I'm here to ask you some questions about Caleb McCord."

Day
90
Ninety

Caleb was the first to call me two days later. One of the nurses had given him a phone. He would be out of the hospital by that evening.

I didn't know how to tell him about the detective. Should Caleb know that the cops were asking questions about him? Lawrence Powers' interrogation had been strange for me. He wanted to know how long I had been dating Caleb and if he portrayed any strange behavior.

"He's a cool guy," I said to him. "Caleb has always been sweet to me."

Then his gaze fell on the bruises on my wrist. "You hurt yourself, Miss Grace?"

"Yes," I quickly replied, covering my wrist with the sleeve of my shirt. "It was an accident at home. I should have been watching the stairs."

He nodded, jotted something down in his notebook, and said to me, "Thanks for your time. I guess I'll be seeing you around. I still have some things to discuss with you."

"Did Caleb do something wrong?" I asked the officer.

He just responded with a beam. "Not at all."

I could still feel his eyes on me as I backed out of the hospital's parking lot. I had a sinking feeling the cops knew something about my relationship with Caleb. Did they know about the cabin? Did they know that, apart from being abused by Caleb, he had locked me up for days and almost killed me?

I didn't want anyone to know about it, not even the cops. The doctor at the hospital where I had managed to drive to, after running from Caleb, hadn't bothered to ask where I got the wounds from. She tried to help though, but I wasn't ready to talk about it.

Only Lauren and my parents. The ones who birthed me wouldn't really care if I was run over by a train. Although my mother had tried to show some sympathy, it felt very pretentious to me. Lauren cared, and I had asked her not to tell anyone about the beatings. Had she been talking to the cops?

However, I didn't tell Caleb about the detective. It was for the best if he didn't know. I wanted him to recover and go back to being the sweet Caleb I had fallen for.

I picked him up in the evening, much to the disapproval of Lauren. But she couldn't stop me from driving to the hospital and getting Caleb into my truck.

He had no one, and I seemed to be the only one who cared that he had tried to commit suicide. Caleb couldn't thank me enough, talking about how I meant everything to him.

His place was the same as Lauren and I had left it. I was able to tidy up the house, clearing the scene of his suicidal act. Caleb shouldn't have to see what he had tried to do.

"Are you coming back here?" He asked me as I led him to the sofa in the living room so we could watch a movie together.

I stared at him, unsure of what to say. To be honest, I wanted to return. The place may bear memories of what had transpired between us, but I believed Caleb had changed for good. Maybe his near-death experience had transported him into a realm of truth, the darkness in his heart being pierced by the light of redemption.

I didn't mean it in the religious sense, but I strongly agreed that Caleb's death had made him a different person. From the way he smiled at me to the way he apologized for the simplest things he did, I was driven to tears by the new man before me.

"Lauren is going to kill me."

He lowered his gaze, a sad look spreading across his face.

"I understand if she hates me now, but I want to change. I need her to know that."

"She doesn't want to talk about you."

Then he cradled my free hand in his. The other hand held the TV remote.

"Maybe Lauren isn't as important to me as much as you are." Caleb was pleading with his eyes. "I need you back in my life. I can't do this without you."

I patted the back of his hand.

"I have to think about it."

"Natalie, I'm prepared to go the extra mile to show you how much I mean this. You can't leave me. I won't be able to survive without you.

This wasn't the first time he would be saying these things. Caleb always had the perfect words for me to hear. He knew how to make me see the truth in his eyes even when he was lying.

However, as I looked back at him, the feeling I got did not convince me that he was lying. Caleb McCord appeared to be telling the truth.

"When I stopped breathing," Caleb continued. "I saw myself in a different place. I saw that I had hurt you a lot, and it broke me. Now that I have been given a second chance, I want to make it up to you."

I placed a hand on his cheek.

"I forgive you, Caleb."

His response came as a kiss. As his lips connected with mine, I felt wonderful again, holding onto the passion that flooded me. His kiss ignited a fire in me, one that had been doused out for a while now. Caleb loved me, and I wanted him in my life forever.

When he broke the kiss, Caleb's magic had overpowered me again. If he had told me to pack my bags at that moment, I would've.

"Don't hate me," he said. "I would try to kill myself again."

"No, no, don't say that," I quickly answered.

"You can't be sure I won't try doing that if you don't come back."

He meant it. The way he was looking at me showed it all. Caleb could possibly devise a faster way to kill himself. This time around, I would not be able to save him.

"I'll be back," I finally told him. "First thing in the morning, I'll bring back my stuff."

A smile appeared on his face. Caleb leaned in again and kissed me.

"Thank you, Natalie. Thank you."

Day
92
Ninety-Two

I was running because, if I stopped, he would find me and berate me again, hitting me with those hands that once made me feel safe.

The rain blinded me as I fought my way through it, the frigid raindrops digging into my subtle skin while the storm roared in my ears as if I had somehow offended the gods of the storms and not my callous fiancé.

I counted from one to thirty as I kept running, knowing fully well that somewhere close to twenty-five, Lauren's room was nearby. Glancing behind me, even in the merciless torrent, it was almost as if I could see his formidable shape, overtaking me and pinning me to the wet ground while he used his fingers to tear my skin. He tore me apart every single time. I couldn't save myself.

Unfocused, I tripped on something, possibly a stone, and found my face buried in the slobber.

"Please, don't hurt me!"

I yelled above the sound of the rain, raising my hand above my head, but no rough hands grabbed me, neither did I feel punches knocking the breath out of me.

It was just my imagination. Scrambling to my feet and feeling the mud heavy on my face but slowly falling away as the rain washed it, I continued my journey and soon found my best friend's house.

But it wasn't the dorm at the college. It was a small bungalow the size of two cabins roughly joined. The whole house was made of wood, creaking loudly as the storm raged against it.

I wondered how it could still stay rooted and hadn't, by now, been the storm's dinner, swirling helplessly into its wide yawn. That thought must have come, possibly, from how much the wooden windows rattled and the house itself shook.

"Lauren! Lauren! Help me!" I knocked on the door, but the storm must have drowned out my voice.

Lauren was the only one who could save me. She had warned me about this beast, but her pleas had fallen on deaf ears. How could I protect myself now? How could I run and know that he couldn't get to me anymore?

I made the mistake of looking behind me. From afar, the raindrops casting a mist before my eyes, I made out an incorporeal shape, wading its way toward me. No human moved like that and so fast. I couldn't make out his face, the stubble growing into snakes that hissed at me.

In no time, he would get to me. I would give in to the pain he loved to bring upon me. My fiancé was the creator of pain, and I was only his creature meant to bask in it.

This time around, I knocked harder on the door, hearing the disembodied creature close in, its cry of rage piercing my eardrums. He was angry that I had left him. I had disobeyed his orders, and he wanted me to pay.

At the last minute, the door flung open. Someone stood before me, a lamp dangling from her hold, but it wasn't Lauren. It was a woman with hollow eyes that burned with fire, her wrinkled skin melting as though someone had poured an ocean of acid on it. Her mouth was open as though in shock, a forked tongue slowly writhing out of it.

"You have to die!" She spoke, but her voice sounded as if thousands of demons were speaking through her.

"No, no," I muttered, backing away from her and certain that I would run into the other monster that was waiting to devour me.

"You have to die, Natalie. There is no saving you."

Then she raised her liquefying arm and hurled the lamp at my skull, flames immediately sprouting out of it and burning my face.

"No! Stop it!"

The fire lapped me, racing up my body with such intense pain I fell to my knees, crying in agony.

I wanted it to stop, wanted it to go away, but it didn't. It just burned fiercely, bringing to mind the scene of terrible anguish and burning corpses.

As I stuck one hand out of the fire, hoping to reach for something, or someone, that would take me out of this hell, I heard a burst of cold laughter right above me, digging like icy shards into my heart. It hurt so much, feeling my body burn and my heart freeze at the same time.

"You're mine, Natalie." It was Caleb's voice.

Almost immediately, I was plunged into complete darkness.

"Miss Grace?" A woman was tapping my shoulder.

I jerked out of my slumber, squinting as the glare of the room's lights flooded my vision. It was another nightmare, and I just had it in the waiting room of Buckley's Mental Help.

"Mr. Buckley will see you now."

I thanked her, realized that I had been drooling, and quickly wiped the slobber from my mouth. The woman had seen it but said nothing about it. She didn't want me to feel embarrassed.

"Where is his office?" I asked as I got to my feet, holding my bag close to my chest.

"The last door on your right," she answered.

"Thanks," I said again and went in the direction.

I partially limped, a result of what Caleb had done to me. Oh, that was before the suicide attempt. He had hurt me so much in the knees that I feared I wouldn't be able to walk again. However, I was here, heading to see the face of a man who could help me.

"Mr. Buckley" was etched into a polished door sign as I stood in front of it. I knocked gently but got no reply.

I was on my second knock when the door opened, and a man's face came into view.

"Oh, sorry, I didn't…"

"Come on in," he said, breaking into a friendly smile. "I'm Buckley."

I stepped into his posh office, wondering how a therapist had gotten so rich. On the walls were portraits of beautiful sceneries. I recognized the waterfall at Whitman Park, the very place I had met Caleb several months ago.

"Take a seat," Buckley offered.

Of course, he had a long sofa I could lie on. I didn't want to do that. I just wanted to sit, tell him my problems, and get the hell out of there.

Mr. Buckley was a fat man who seemed to smile a lot. Behind his circle-rimmed glasses, his gaze was at times serious, peering into my soul as if he could read my thoughts.

"So, what brings you in here?" he asked, setting a notepad on his lap.

That seemed to be a very weird question for a therapist. He definitely knew why I was there.

"To get help," I responded with a chuckle, hoping I didn't sound rude.

"Of course." Mr. Buckley was smiling again. "I know that, but *why* are you here? We do have to start from somewhere, don't we?"

I stared at the waterfall portrait in front of him and didn't know where to begin. Should I start with Josh, or start from the very beginning, where my problems had stemmed from? I meant, my parents. They started the abuse, and it must have been why fate kept pushing me to people who loved to hurt me.

You're created for pain, Natalie Grace.

"I really don't know where to begin," I confessed to the therapist.

He looked at me for a few seconds and asked, "What do you love doing, Miss Grace?"

"Pardon?"

"What are your hobbies? What makes you relax when you're tense?"

To be honest, my mind could only go to music. On nights when I cried and thought about how terrible my life was, music filtering into my ears, taking me out of my misery, did the magic. I could sleep all my problems off with the pods still in my ears.

"Music," I told him.

"Good," Mr. Buckley responded and rose to his feet.

He walked over to an old stereo on his shelf. I didn't know people still used old gadgets like that.

"So, you don't mind if I play whatever you like?"

I chuckled again. "You don't know what I like."

"See, Miss Grace, I took this job because I figured out my ability to read people. I understand them and know the very things they like. Want to give me a try?"

I glanced incredulously at him. "Of course. What music do I like?"

"I'll say jazz," said Mr. Buckley. "You're the sort of woman who loves calm music, songs capable of comforting you."

A tear nearly dropped from my eye. He was right. Mr. Buckley had correctly guessed my favorite genre of music. Had this happened because he could see the hurt I bore?

"Jazz," came my reply. "That's it."

After he put in jazz for me, steadily instilling bliss in me, Mr. Buckley took his seat and asked his question again.

"Caleb. That's his name," I started.

Mr. Buckley wrote something down. "Who is he to you?"

I could have answered, but I wanted to be sure about something first. "Everything I tell you here, are they going to stay between us?"

"There is absolute confidentiality in this business, Miss Grace. Yes, everything stays between us."

"Okay."

"Why don't you relax?"

He meant lying down on his couch. I thought about it. It wasn't a bad idea.

As I settled in, I heard Mr. Buckley say, "So, who is Caleb to you?"

I stared at my fingers. "The man I love."

"How much do you love him?"

"Very much. I want to spend the rest of my life with him."

"So, did Caleb ask you to come here, or did he make you come here?"

I sighed deeply. This was the part I didn't like to talk about. Even with the jazz playing, I wanted to keep Caleb's problem a secret.

"Actually, I found your flyer on my windshield."

Mr. Buckley gave a soft laugh. "Sorry about that. We needed to let people know about us."

"We?" I was facing him now, my back still on the sofa.

I knew Mr. Buckley was trying to be patient with me by allowing my digression. However, the session was for an hour, and I would have to start answering his question whether I liked it or not.

"Well, the woman you met outside is my wife. Her name is Gabriella. We started this practice together."

"Why? You like people talking about their problems to you?"

A smile just stretched across the therapist's face.

"I believe that's a question I'll answer during one of our sessions. But we aren't here for me, are we? Let's talk about you, Natalie. Let's talk about you and Caleb."

I turned to stare at the whitewashed ceiling. It reminded me of Caleb's place. I had moved into the house two days ago, and Caleb had been so nice that he made me breakfast, lunch, *and* dinner.

However, he didn't know about my trip down here. I hadn't discussed it with him. I didn't know what he would think about it.

"He loves me," I replied.

"Is that what he tells you?"

I nodded. "He tells me every day."

Mr. Buckley was scribbling into his notepad so fast that I didn't think it was even humanly possible. I didn't know why that interested him.

"How does he show that he loves you?"

Caleb had different love languages. It was like several people living in one person. Sometimes, he was sweet and caring, promising me that I was all that mattered to him. Other days, he insulted me, hitting and slapping me while he claimed he did it out of love.

"He buys me things and takes me out," I said, and my voice began to break. "And then he hurts me because he cares."

Mr. Buckley stopped writing. He was looking at me now. I could tell because I was staring back at him, too.

"Hurts you? How?"

I didn't answer. Mr. Buckley closed his pad. Was it a sign of frustration? That, I couldn't tell.

"Miss Grace, I can't help you if you tell me nothing. I need to know how Caleb hurts you."

I sat up straight. "He's broken. My fiancé is broken. I just need to save him."

"Looks like you need to be saved yourself. Forget about him for now, and focus on yourself."

I shook my head. "This isn't working. I came here so you could tell me how to save him."

"That's not how this works, Miss Grace."

But I was already on my feet. I took my bag and headed for the door.

"Sorry for wasting your time."

"Miss Grace, wait," the therapist called, and I stopped to hear him out, my hand hovering over the doorknob.

"You asked why my wife and I started this practice, and I'm ready to give you an answer now."

I turned around to face him. He was still seated, but his legs were now crossed.

"We started it because of our son, Jordan. My son was the most vibrant teenager you would ever meet.

He was so full of life that he brought smiles on the faces of everyone he encountered."

Mr. Buckley was about to tell his story. I had chosen not to tell him mine, but here he was, narrating the life of his son.

"One day, he changed. Gabriella and I should have seen it earlier, but we chose to turn a blind eye. We saw him as a young boy going through different phases of life. But Jordan was depressed. He was so full of gloom that one morning, he woke up and went to the Whitman waterfall, where he fell headlong into the water and died."

I almost let out a gasp. Mr. Buckley's son had committed suicide? But how was he still so happy? How come he wore that perfect smile as if his son wasn't six feet underground?

"You see that portrait?" He was pointing at the Whitman picture. "I took it on the day he died and hung it here. It reminds me every morning of my purpose in life. To never let another person end up like Jordan."

Silence followed the sad story. I had no idea what to say. The only misery I felt came from being broken by those who should have molded me. I had never experienced the pain of losing someone dear to me.

"Mr. Buckley," I said, walking back to the couch and taking my seat. "I'm sorry to hear about that."

His charming smile was back. "Oh, don't worry. I have come to accept my destiny. I don't know if you're ready to do that, too."

I was. I wanted to live past this.

"I am." That was my answer, and I told him all about Caleb.

Day
96
Ninety-Six

Four days later, I went to Lauren's birthday party.

She didn't throw a big party, just a small one in her dorm with a few of our mutual friends invited. I had told Caleb about it, and he asked to come.

"Lauren doesn't like you," I told him as I got dressed. "It might not be a good idea."

Caleb came to hug me from behind, planting a kiss on my neck. "You look beautiful."

I blushed. "Thanks."

It's been five days now without any sort of argument or desire to hit me. I was starting to believe Caleb's promise. He smiled often, and he rarely talked about his unemployment.

"You're my alluring angel," he said again, this time, placing his hands on my breasts.

"Alright, such sweet words, but I have to go."

Caleb reluctantly let me go. As I walked out of the room, he was still watching me, which creeped me out.

My therapy with Mr. Buckley had gone well, but it only made me realize how scary Caleb was. I loved him but, at the same time, feared him.

If Caleb had said I looked beautiful, then Lauren was absolutely stunning. As soon as my best friend saw me, she raced toward me in her skimpy black gown with diamond studs on it. Her hair had been styled into a French weave, so she looked like some classy female billionaire.

"You made it," Lauren cried.

"Yes, I did," I said, hugging her tightly. "Gosh, Lauren, you look gorgeous."

"I know, right?" Lauren responded, turning around so I could have a better look at her. "The dress is new. You look beautiful, too. What's that? A new lipstick?"

"It's strawberry. Elena."

"Elena?" Lauren was surprised. "That's expensive."

I didn't know how to tell her that Caleb bought it for me. Somehow, he knew Elena Jacobs, the owner and CEO of Elena Beauty, one of the best makeup companies in the state. It had been a great surprise, but I didn't bother to ask how he knew her. I wanted to stay out of Caleb's past. Mr. Buckley had advised me of that.

"Things happen."

Lauren put my hand on her chest, hugging it fondly, "I'm happy that you're happy."

"Thanks."

"I would like you to meet someone," Lauren told me. "His name is Justin. A very cool guy."

She pulled me into the room where her friends had gathered. I recognized every one of them except a tall blonde guy in jeans. He was very attractive, possessing the charming facial features of Caleb.

However, before we got to him, I pulled away from Lauren.

"Why do I have to meet this guy?"

Lauren was eyeing me. "Because he's a cool guy. And super handsome."

"I'm really not keen on meeting new people."

I didn't want to hurt Lauren's feelings, but to be candid, my problem with Caleb had started with her. If she hadn't forced me into getting over Josh, maybe my life wouldn't have been this messy.

"I see," Lauren said.

She stopped holding me.

"Lauren," I started to say to her, but then her eyebrows furrowed into a frown.

"What's he doing here?"

I turned around to see who she was talking about. It was Caleb! What was he *really* doing here?

"I'm sorry," I quickly apologized. "I told him not to come. I'll be back."

When I got to Caleb, he was already chatting with a friend of Lauren's, Brenda.

"Hey, babe," Caleb called me. "Meet Brenda. She's very friendly, and she's a zoologist."

I fixed Brenda a smile. "I know that. Caleb, what are you doing here?"

His smile vanished, followed by a cold look. Brenda seemed to have noticed the reaction. She left right away.

"It's your friend's birthday party. Why can't I be here?"

I lowered my voice. "She doesn't want you here. I told you that."

I saw him grit, the same way he did any time he got angry and came at me. But he stayed rooted where he was, just staring at me with eyes that revealed his rage. I must have struck a nerve.

"Are you just going to let your friend not invite me to her party?"

"It's *her* party, Caleb. Not mine."

"I don't want you here." Lauren had now gotten behind us.

This was bad, really bad. I didn't want my best friend to have a face-off with my fiancé. It would turn into a bitter quarrel.

"Hello, Lauren." Caleb's polite smile was back on his face. "Nice party you have here."

"Get your bullshit out of here," Lauren responded, raising her voice. "I know who you really are, and my friend doesn't need you in her life."

"Lauren," I begged, trying to hold her. "Don't make a scene."

Lauren slapped my hand away. I didn't want her to tell everyone what I was dealing with, but Lauren seemed to be ready to do that. Caleb, on the other hand, appeared calm. If anyone had walked in on them, they would think Lauren was the hot-tempered one.

"You don't have to keep going back to him. He's too toxic for you, Natalie. Why can't you see that?"

"Lauren, what do you know about Pink Alley?" came Caleb's voice.

As soon as he said that, the furious look on Lauren's face disappeared, followed by a look of horror. You would think she had just seen a ghost.

"What? How did you…?"

Caleb was smirking. "See, we all have secrets."

I glanced at my friend, expecting her to say something. Somehow, she had lost the ability to speak. The party had quiet down, all eyes on Lauren.

"I don't know what you're talking about," she stuttered, but it was clearly a lie.

Caleb moved closer to her, the smirk refusing to leave his face.

"Lauren, I'm going to keep your secret if you keep mine. Happy Birthday."

With that, he walked out of the party, possibly feeling like a hero who had just saved the day. Lauren refused to look at me.

"What's that about? What's Pink Alley?" I asked her.

"Not important," she said and raced out of the party.

I tried to follow her but couldn't find out where she had gone to. Lauren had been crying when she left me. The Pink Alley business must have brought bad memories for her.

When I got to my truck, Caleb was already waiting for me. A cigarette in his mouth. He puffed into the air as I approached, watching me with eyes that showed mischief. My fiancé was scaring me again.

"You're done?" he asked.

"No," I replied. "Lauren ran out. I think the party ended."

Caleb nodded, appearing to have enjoyed that news. "Come on, let's go home."

"I have to look for Lauren."

"Now!"

His sudden outburst caused me to jerk. If I tried to disobey him, I knew what was coming for me. Caleb had talked about changing. Was that even true?

"Okay," I said and got into the truck with him.

I had no choice. Caleb was everything to me.

The next day, I went to the grocery store to shop for Caleb. That was where I met Detective Lawrence Powers again. This time around, he was with a short woman with flaming red hair.

From the way she looked, I could have sworn she was scared of something. Her eyes seemed to dart everywhere, and the way her hand gripped the strap of her bag, I noticed she was nervous.

"Miss Grace," greeted the detective. "How have you been?"

I pushed the grocery basket in front of me. This wasn't the time to talk to the detective. In fact, I didn't want to ever converse with him. Caleb had spent last night making love to me and promising me that we wouldn't fight again. If he found me talking to the officer, I was sure he would get very angry.

"Detective Powers," I said to him. "I would love to stay and talk, but I can't. I need to get back home."

"Miss Grace, I won't take much of your time," the detective said. "It's about Caleb McCord."

I heard the woman whimper as if the name Caleb made her want to cry. When I glanced at her, she had her head lowered. There was something weird about her.

"I don't have anything to say about him," I replied to the detective. "I told you everything the last time we spoke."

"Maybe my friend here would interest you." He was speaking about the woman. "Miss Grace, meet Mandy Halliday."

That was when I stopped in my tracks, my hands gripping the handle of the basket as if I would snap it into two. Did the detective just say Mandy Halliday? As in Caleb's former wife?

I spun to look at her again, this time around, my face possibly revealing my fright. How in the world was she alive? When Caleb had talked about making her disappear, I thought he meant he had her killed. What if making her disappear meant she went away, somewhere far away from him?

"I see you have heard about her." The detective had seen the look on my face. "What did Caleb tell you about Mandy?"

But I ignored him. I was more interested in the redhead in front of me.

"Mandy? You're Mandy?"

The woman stammered as she said, "I didn't...I didn't want to come here. Please... don't...tell Caleb you met me."

I blinked back tears. This woman wasn't different from me. She was utterly scared of Caleb. What had he done to her?

"Miss Halliday," Detective Lawrence said to her. "It's fine. Caleb doesn't know about this meeting."

"Then we have to hurry up. I don't want to risk... risk it."

"Miss Grace?" The detective now had a grin on his face. "How about we all go for a drink?"

The detective picked a restaurant not far from the grocery store.

Although I didn't ask for a drink, the detective ordered a cup of coffee for me, one for Mandy, and a soda for himself. I couldn't get my eyes off Mandy. Even as she raised the cup to her lips, I could see her tremble. She seemed ready to get the hell out of here.

I sipped my coffee too and waited for the detective to do the introduction. It wasn't my job to go first. The officer had called for this meeting, and he would handle it.

"So, Miss Grace, tell us what you know about Mandy," said the detective.

I thought about what to say. It would be pointless lying to the detective. He wanted me to meet Mandy for a reason. As for me, I had a billion questions to ask her.

When Caleb had told me about his ex-wife, it sounded like the truth. Now, I was beginning to see what a big liar he was. He had even lied about his father making Mandy disappear. When exactly had Caleb ever told me the truth? I couldn't tell.

"He said she disappeared," I started. "Maybe I got it all wrong. I thought he…"

"Killed her?" The detective finished my statement when he realized I wasn't ready to talk again. "You can always tell me everything, Miss Grace."

"I really don't know," I answered. "That was what he told me."

"Well, as you can see, she isn't dead," added Detective Lawrence. "But she has a lot to say, which I think is the same for you."

"May I ask, Detective Powers, why you're so interested in Caleb?" That was me.

I saw him glance at Mandy, who had her head lowered again as though she found something interesting in her coffee cup. The only thing the detective told me was that he was investigating Caleb because there was something peculiar about him. I didn't believe him, and the detective could see it now.

"A few years ago, I met Mandy Halliday in a hospital ward, and she told me a lot of things about Caleb McCord. I didn't believe her at first because she had no evidence. Although I could see the bruises and wounds, but you know how people can be. I thought Mandy was only out to pin a crime on the son of a senator."

I had wounds and bruises I was hiding from a lot of people. So, I would have believed Mandy if she had told me that years ago. No one was out to incriminate Caleb. He was indeed troubled and abusive.

"When did you start to believe her?"

"One night, when she called my phone and claimed some men had kidnapped her from her home and tried to kill her, but she escaped. I drove to where she was and took her back home. Mandy was a total mess. A day before, Caleb had beaten her, broken her jaw, and refused to take her to the hospital. Then he tried to nurse her, and when

Mandy asked him not to, he flared up again and stormed out of the house."

The unstable behavior! He had done that with Mandy, too. It was impossible to tell who or what Caleb even liked.

"Somehow, seeing her cry and wounded in my house, I believed her. Mandy said it was a mistake that she married him. She foolishly thought that she was in love and endured his crazy attitude because Caleb was manipulative. His father kept covering up his crimes. I think he hired some people to abduct Mandy."

Mandy was right about the manipulative part. Caleb knew how to make me stay. He could hurt me for days, and I would keep running back to him. That was how well he controlled me.

I nodded. "He said his father made Mandy disappear. But why didn't you do something about it? Why didn't you take up a case against him?"

Mandy blew her nose. I didn't even know when she started to cry.

"There was no evidence, Miss Grace," said the detective on her behalf. "That was why I approached you. If you could get me proof that Caleb had hurt you, then…"

"I can't do that," I interrupted. "I'm sorry."

"You don't have to be scared of him, Miss Grace," continued the officer. "He doesn't have to know anything. Save yourself, Natalie. Save yourself from this man."

I wish I could do that, but I couldn't. A part of me still wanted to be with Caleb. A part of me hoped that underneath his beastly character, I would find his sweet self, yearning to be rescued.

"You're wrong, Detective Lawrence," I said to him. "Caleb doesn't hurt me."

"That was what I told myself, too," Mandy spoke for the first time since we entered the restaurant.

Her voice trembled just as her hand fiddled with her necklace.

"At first, I thought he was bothered by something. I waited for him to change. I believed that he would change. Caleb said the same thing, too. He said he hated hurting me, and I trusted him. But he wouldn't stop."

Her voice was breaking as she resumed crying. If I wasn't attentive to what she was saying or found it really relatable, I wouldn't have heard her over the hiccups and sniffling.

"Then the situation got worse. Caleb woke up one morning and placed a hot iron on my back. I still have the scar. He said it was because I snored in my sleep, and it bothered him."

That was horrible. But it was almost the same as my situation. Caleb had tried to drown me, and he enjoyed the sight of me thrashing about in the water.

"Then he would take care of my wounds and tell me he was sorry. I would go back to him because I had no one else. He was genuinely romantic when he wanted to be."

"You married him when you were eighteen?" I cut in to ask that question.

Mandy nodded. "We were young and in love. Caleb was my world. He meant everything to me. His father once tried to dissuade me from marrying him, but I didn't listen."

"I think the senator knew about his son's psychotic disorder," added the detective.

I was still going to ask the cop about Caleb's father, but not now. I wanted Mandy to finish her story.

"What was the last straw that broke the camel's back?" That was me.

"When he slept with my best friend on our bed," Mandy answered. "I came back from work to find them on it. That changed everything because I couldn't believe he would do that to me. He knew how much I loved my friend."

So, Caleb *had* slept with other women while he was married to Mandy? That wasn't a surprise, though. I couldn't count the many women he had fucked in the same bed we shared.

"Caleb sent my friend home and descended on me. The beating was more this time. He used anything within his reach to inflict wounds on me. When he smashed the bedside lamp against my head, I felt my jaw shift. Caleb saw it too and stopped. Then he tried to nurse me like he always did. I couldn't take it this time around. So, I asked him to leave. Caleb was pissed off and called his father. That same night, strangers broke into our home a few hours after Caleb left for vacation and kidnapped me."

"How did you escape?"

"They put me in a car's trunk and forgot to lock it. I found my way out and ran as far away as possible from them. When I called Lawrence, I couldn't even speak. My jaw was broken, and I was scared as hell."

Damn, she had gone through all that? It made me wonder what Caleb had in store for me. What would happen if he got to beat me like he did to Mandy? Would he break my jaw or disfigure my face?

"What happened to Caleb's father?" I asked.

It almost seemed as if I was trying to avoid any talk of getting the detective evidence of Caleb beating the shit out of me. Maybe I was.

"No one knows," replied Detective Lawrence. "The whole country woke up to the news of him gone."

Somehow, my mind told me something had happened to the man. What if he had gotten tired of covering up for Caleb, and the dude had gotten rid of him? It wouldn't be a surprise.

"If you need any proof, you should find his father," I told the detective and made them leave.

Detective Lawrence rose to his feet. "His father? That's a dead end. Besides, I don't think the man would be inclined toward testifying against his own son."

"And you want *me* to do it?"

"Don't you want to make him pay for what he's been doing to you?"

"He doesn't hurt me!" I insisted.

"I'm not a fool, Miss Grace. I see how you hide the scars and bruises. I know a scared woman when I see one. You're no different from Mandy here. Look what he did to her! He beat her so much that she lost their baby. She was pregnant at the time."

That was shocking. Mandy hadn't told me about that. All of a sudden, I felt weak. The fear of losing my child by the hands of Caleb overpowered me. I wasn't pregnant, but what if I ended up carrying his child? What if he turns me barren like Mandy?

"Yes, Miss Grace," continued the detective. "That is how monstrous Caleb McCord is. It's up to you to help me put him behind bars."

That was when I broke down and began to cry.

Day
102
One Hundred Two

It's been days now, and Caleb and I had yet to fight.

That was strange of him, and with every minute I spent with him in the house, I expected him to wake up one morning and start to beat me as usual. The detective had asked me to record any of our disagreements. I didn't have the courage to pick up my phone to risk having my face pushed in again.

It would come. Somehow, I was sure of it, and that was because I knew it was impossible to get Caleb to truly change. However, he was starting to prove me wrong these days.

Today, I was sitting in his expansive living room, getting off a call with Lauren as soon as he walked inside. She wanted to know if I would be at the college dinner party. I had no time for any of that now. The truth was that, I had this fear that if I ended up going to one, a random person would point out the bruises I had been concealing, and I would break down into tears again.

But that wasn't my greatest fear. I still couldn't believe Caleb had allowed his father to take away Mandy, his wife. There was no doubt what he would do to me if he found out I had talked to her. Like everyone else, Caleb probably thought his wife was dead.

"Hey," he said to me and flopped down on the sofa.

"Hey," I greeted back.

I watched him grab the remote and start to go through channels, unsure of what to watch. There was something I had been trying to ask him, but for some reason, my mind warned me not to. Caleb was dangerous. He got angry when I asked him things.

However, today, I wanted to do it. Whatever reaction I would get from him, it would certainly be enough proof to give the detective.

I tapped the screen of my phone and went to voice recorder. That felt like a perfect way to record the conversation I was about to have with him. I doubted camera recording would have been easy for me, considering I would have to place it in a position that would film the entire thing. He would have suspected.

After I began to record, I placed the phone between us. Caleb's gaze was glued to the TV screen. He was now watching the highlights of a football match.

"Caleb?" I started.

"Yes?"

"You said something at Lauren's birthday, and I want to ask you about it."

"Okay."

It was about Pink Alley. Ever since he said that, Lauren had been acting strange. It was as though Caleb knew something about her that I didn't.

"What's Pink Alley?" I asked.

Caleb didn't look at me when he answered. "Nothing."

"Please, Caleb," I pleaded. "Lauren is my friend. I need to know if she's in trouble or not."

A vein thickened in his neck. It was coming. Caleb was starting to feel enraged. I prayed my phone was still recording.

"Why are you asking me? Ask your friend."

"She's not ready to talk. I thought you could tell me since…"

"Since what, Natalie?" He snapped. "I am not telling you anything. Ask your best friend."

I tried to push further, but Caleb had heard enough of it. He turned off the TV, rose to his feet, and walked out of the room.

That was a disappointment. He had made no effort to hurt me. I took my phone and deleted the recording. That wasn't enough to prove anything.

What if Caleb *had* seriously changed, and I was only trying to look for something that was no longer there? If this was real, then I loved it.

I didn't even know when I began to cry. Hot tears flowed down my cheeks as I tried to embrace the possibility of a new Caleb McCord.

"Please," I said, staring up at the ceiling. "Let this be real."

I had no idea who I was praying to, but at that moment, my mind went to Lauren's God. The pastor had talked about him being a miraculous God. Caleb's decision not to beat me was indeed a miracle.

Just then, Caleb returned. I had not been expecting him, so a loud gasp escaped from my lips when I saw him storming toward me, eyes gleaming with rage.

A painful slap tore across my cheek, making me fall back so that my neck hit the sofa. Caleb had hit me!

"Don't you ever ask me to talk about your friend! She's a bitch! You're a bitch!"

With that, he went out of the house, taking his car keys with him. I just lied face up on the sofa, staring at the ceiling and trying to process what had just happened.

I had fooled myself. No miracle had occurred. Caleb was still the monster he had revealed to me, and I didn't have it on record.

The following day, I called Detective Lawrence. He was pleased to hear my voice.

"Miss Grace," he said. "Good to hear your voice."

"He's going to kill me," was my first reply.

"What?"

I could almost picture the detective's look of worry. I didn't need anyone to be concerned about me. I had brought this upon myself.

"Are you okay? Should I send the cops over?"

"I'm good," I answered. "We got into a fight yesterday, but I didn't have time to record."

Detective Lawrence's voice deepened. "Are you fine, Miss Grace?"

"I think Cole Watkins might have answers."

There was a pause. Maybe the detective was jotting the name down.

"Who is Cole Watkins?"

"He is Caleb's friend and works in a psychiatric hospital."

I didn't want to go into details of how I found out about Cole and where he worked. The important thing was, I knew where he worked.

"Are you sure this man is going to talk about his friend?"

"He once advised me to save myself. He knows something."

"Alright," said the detective. "Let's pay him a visit this afternoon, shall we?"

Cole Watkins wasn't in his office by the time we arrived, but his secretary led us to the cafeteria where he was devouring a plate of hamburgers. Cole smiled as he saw me, but he had no idea that the man walking beside me was a police officer.

"Natalie," he greeted. "And you're?"

"Detective Lawrence Powers," the man introduced himself, shoving a badge in his face.

Cole's smile vanished. He looked up at me as though I had betrayed him.

"Can we sit with you?" asked Detective Lawrence.

"Of course," replied Cole, but his voice faltered for a brief second.

"Cole," I said to him after taking my seat. "I had to do it. Look at my face."

This time around, I didn't bother to conceal the bruise on my cheek from where Caleb had slapped me yesterday. Ever since I met Mandy, something had changed in me.

I was no longer interested in enduring what Caleb had been doing to me. It was as if I wanted the whole world to see him for what he really was.

"Caleb hurt me again. I'm tired of everything," I added.

Cole didn't say a word to me. I had a strong belief that he was scared to talk, especially in front of a police officer.

"You know about this, don't you?" asked Detective Lawrence.

"I don't know what you're talking about," Cole said with a straight face.

Detective Lawrence just chuckled. "She did say you're going to be a tough one. I believe you know your friend, Caleb, is committing a crime. If you don't tell me everything you know about him, that's technically abetting him in his crime."

"I am abetting no one. You have no proof."

"Really, Mr. Watkins?" said the detective. "You think I have no proof? Why would I be here trying to gather testifiers if I have no proof? Do you want me to play the recording on my phone? Do you want to hear how monstrous the guy you're protecting is?"

The detective had just lied, but I knew about it. This was only a means to persuade Cole to talk. I could see that it was working. After Cole heard about a recording, that seemed to rattle him.

"Aren't you heartless if you don't care about this poor woman here? He tried to drown her, Mr. Watkins. He fucking locked her up in a room after breaking her ankles and hitting her head. She could have died, and you would have had to live with the guilt of knowing you could have done something to save her."

Cole was trembling. He had to shift his plate away from him, relaxing his hands on the table. It was only a matter of time before he spilled his guts.

"I am giving you a chance to save this woman, Mr. Watkins. Look into her eyes and feel her pain. Understand the misery she is passing through, and stop trying to cover up for Mr. McCord. He is a monster, and you know it!"

"You're right. He *is* a monster!" confessed Cole. "I am sorry for everything, Natalie. But I told you to save yourself. I warned you not to go back to him."

"He is only going to forget about me and move onto the next person," I blurted out. "That's my fear, Cole. He's going to love someone else and hurt her like he did to me. Who knows? Maybe kill her, and her blood would be on me. I don't want that to happen. This has to stop."

I was now crying, breath trembling from remembering my recent nightmares. They started after I met Mandy. In each of them, I saw the body of an innocent girl that had been crushed by Caleb.

Mandy would then appear behind me and say, "You did this to her, Natalie. I'm not innocent, either. We could have stopped it."

That was the last thing I would ever do – allow someone else to be hurt by Caleb. Whatever demons he was fighting, he needed to be locked up, fighting them in solitary confinement.

"Do you know about his former wife, Mandy?" The detective asked Cole.

"Yes," he answered. "But she died a long time ago."

"Was that what he told you?"

Cole hesitated before he said, "To be honest, I didn't believe him, but there was no record of her, so I stopped searching."

"Mandy is alive, Mr. Watkins, but he tried to get rid of her. She also suffered the same fate as Miss

Grace, even worse. I have been in charge of her protection for many years now."

Cole was genuinely surprised. "I didn't know he did it to someone else."

"Which is exactly Miss Grace's point. Caleb is a crazy man. God knows how many women he has done this to, but they don't have the courage to talk. When I met Mandy, I started to investigate Caleb, but it seemed that most of his relationships after Mandy were secret ones. That was until Miss Grace's happened. This is the second open relationship he has ever had."

"I know," Cole replied. "Caleb told me he wanted to start fresh, and I was happy for him. He said he had fallen in love with Natalie and that he saw a future with her."

Under normal circumstances, I would have been glad to hear that. But everything was wrong now. I didn't want to have a future with Caleb. He would be the death of me before I ever get the chance to live that future.

"I thought that it was the right decision for him," Cole continued. "He was about to lose everything, and Caleb thought that he would die. He was so pessimistic that I didn't know how to save him."

"Wait, let's start from the beginning," said Detective Lawrence, fishing out his notepad. "How do you know Caleb McCord?"

Cole Watkins sighed and proceeded to tell us a very disturbing story.

Day
105
One Hundred Five

According to Mr. Buckley, meeting new people was a great step in getting my life back.

But they weren't just new people. They were people like me, men and women who had endured, or were still in, abusive relationships.

"Our next meeting is this evening," Mr. Buckley had told me. "Would you like to join us?"

To be honest, ever since I started attending the therapeutic sessions, my mind had been at peace. Although it was sometimes rattled by the craziness of Caleb, I could confidently say that Buckley's Mental Help had worked well for me. Every time I stepped into the office, I was always eager to listen to jazz music and answer the therapist's questions.

Today, however, I was disappointed because Mr. Buckley said there would be no session. He wanted me to join the meeting he had with his other clients.

"Sure. What time is it?"

"6pm. Can you make it?"

I nodded. "I can."

Then he studied me for a while. "Would Caleb let you leave the house?"

"Well, he's been in a good mood these days. His football team won. I don't think it would be a problem coming to the meeting."

Mr. Buckley smiled. "Good."

By the time it was six in the evening, I took my bag and proceeded to leave the house. Caleb was in the kitchen, humming happily to himself. My plan was to walk out of the house without having to explain where I was going. He still had no idea I was meeting a therapist.

"Where are you going?"

Suddenly, Caleb was behind me, asking me that question. My hand froze over the doorknob.

"Shit!" I silently cursed.

"I said, where are you going?" he asked again.

Slowly, I turned around, a huge smile plastered on my face.

"I'm going to my parents'. My mom wants me to meet a friend of hers."

Caleb was standing in front of the kitchen's entrance, a spatula in his hand. It would be wise not to infuriate him. He could easily hit me with the spatula, and that would be nasty.

"You don't like your mother's friends," he reminded me with an eyebrow raised.

"I like this one," I lied again. "Not all of them are bad."

That was when he began to move closer to me. I tried to remain where I was, studying Caleb's eyes. The fastest way to tell if he was angry was by looking into his eyes. His emotions always reflected in them.

"Are you cheating on me?"

"What?" I said with a nervous chuckle. "No. I would never do that."

Then Caleb stopped walking toward me. He folded his arms and said, "Then where do you go every Monday and Thursday?"

"Somewhere," I answered, then realized it wasn't a good reply.

My fiancé was now in front of me. He was so close that I feared he could hear my heart pounding in my chest. Maybe my answer had enraged him; I wasn't sure. But Caleb raised his hand and, as I took a step back in fright, touched my hair. I couldn't believe it. The guy was stroking my hair, not hitting me.

"You don't have to lie to me," he said.

I swallowed hard. "I'm not."

There was something magnetic about his touch. It was almost as though I wanted to reach for him and be safe in his arms again, just like how I had felt before he transformed into a monster. Those days, he made me happy. He made me feel like a woman.

Without warning, Caleb pulled my face toward him and gave me a long kiss. The contact awakened a lost passion in me, flooding me with the burning desire of having him right there in front of the door. His hand went to my breast at the same time, squeezing the one on the left.

What was Caleb doing to me? All of a sudden, I wanted to confess everything to him. From the visits to Buckley Mental Help to the plans Detective Lawrence had in store for him; I wanted Caleb to know everything.

Just as I was giving in to the passionate kiss, Caleb pulled away and looked into my eyes. They bore this feeling of warmth that almost made me cry. I had missed the good Caleb.

"So, where are you going? Do you want to tell me who you're seeing?

"Caleb, have you forgotten I *am* still a college student? Don't be silly. I would never cheat on you."

Caleb appeared disappointed. He probably thought the kiss would work its magic. It almost did.

"Okay, but be back before midnight," he finally said.

I breathed an inaudible sigh of relief. He was letting me go.

"I'll be back before 9."

After I left the house and flagged down a cab, my phone began to ring. It was Mr. Buckley. He had called to remind me of the meeting.

"I'm on my way," I said to him.

The meeting was held in a gym at a high school. Mr. Buckley told me they had picked the venue because it was close to everyone's home. As soon as I got inside the building, I turned off my phone. There would be no time for distractions.

There were five other women in the gym and a man, aside from Mr. Buckley. So, in total, we were eight. I had never met any of them, but they smiled at me as though I wasn't a stranger to them.

"It's so nice of you to join us, Natalie," said Mr. Buckley.

In meetings like this, they usually go by the first name in order to protect everyone's identity. I had no problem with anyone trying to dig up information about me. It wasn't like I was some celebrity.

"This is a safe place for every one of us," continued Mr. Buckley. "Where we can talk about our problems and find bliss in one another. A problem shared is a problem solved. That's what they say. There is no harm or embarrassment in telling others what you have been through. We are all eager to hear your story, Natalie, and you'll be glad that you did."

I didn't know what he meant by that. Was Mr. Buckley saying that sharing my problems with these people would be a thing of joy? How was I supposed to find happiness in my pain? There was no doubt that I would end up crying while telling them my ordeal. I had cried enough this morning in the bathroom just thinking about my shitty life. I had no intention of doing that here also.

"Do you want to go first?" asked Mr. Buckley.

I shook my head. "No."

Mr. Buckley appeared a little disappointed. "Okay. How about you?"

He was pointing to the red-haired woman sitting beside me. When I looked at her, there was a bright smile on her face. I was so sure that whatever she was about to share wouldn't be as bad as mine. That had to be the only reason for her smile.

"Hello, everyone, I'm Lisa," the redhead introduced herself.

"Hi, Lisa," we all repeated.

"I'm a 20-year-old woman who once lived with her father."

She had to be kidding me! Did she just say twenty? If anyone had walked into this room and studied Lisa's face, they would have thought that she was older than I was. I couldn't get my eyes off her wrinkled face and crooked jaw. That reminded me of Mandy and how she couldn't talk because of the broken jaw. Lisa's eyes were sunken as though they would sink into her skull and never re-surface. How in the world was she only twenty?

"I am unemployed, and I don't see myself getting a job in the next ten years," Lisa continued and chuckled.

How did she find that amusing? I couldn't understand.

"My father worked in a construction company and brought food to the table. He had no choice back then. I don't have a mother or a brother who could have possibly helped him bear the burden."

She paused for a few seconds and played with her fingers. I could almost sense her hesitation. No one said anything. They were all waiting for her to talk.

"My father started raping me when I was twelve."

A gasp slipped out from my mouth, and I hardly even knew. The looks of others informed me that I had made a sound. Even Lisa looked up at me, her eyes gathering tears.

"It's okay, Lisa," Mr. Buckley quickly said. "You may continue."

"He did it the first time after I came back from summer camp. I thought it was because he got drunk. He didn't know what he was doing. Then he came back the second time, and he was not drunk. My father knew what he was doing."

What a horrible man! I couldn't even imagine my father sticking his dick in me. I would have killed myself.

"For three years, I kept silent and allowed my body to be desecrated by my father. When I couldn't take it anymore, I decided to report it to our next-door neighbor. She tried to save me and decided to talk to my father. Because I had no evidence, and he warned her to stop poking her nose in other people's business, I couldn't be saved. My father got furious that I had ratted him out. He stopped raping me and began to physically assault me. That man called me names like 'abomination,' 'disgusting piece of trash,' a 'slut,' and so many others."

I had to take back my word. Her problem was a billion times greater than mine. Yes, my parents had assaulted me, but they had never bruised my dignity. They had never shamefully molested me, unlike Lisa. I glanced at the rest of the group and wondered what terrifying story they all had to share.

"He starved me several times and locked me in the basement where I wouldn't see light for days. I remember having to watch a rat lick my sores, and I couldn't do anything because I was too weak. I stopped going to school because of him. He lied to the world that he had decided to home school me. Two years ago, his best friend found out what he was doing to me and reported it to the cops. My father got arrested, and during the ride to the police station, he jumped out of the van in a bid to escape and got crushed by another vehicle. He died, and that was the last time anyone ever assaulted me."

Damn! I wanted to reach for her and hug her for a long time. She had gone through hell. Her past had taken its toll on her, turning her into a woman who looked much older than her age.

"How have you been feeling, Lisa?" asked Mr. Buckley.

Lisa blew her nose. "Happy, I guess. But I'll never be the same. I tried to get into relationships, but no guy ever stayed after listening to my story. He ruined my life, my face, my pride. How is anyone supposed to love me, looking like this?"

"How about Collins, Lisa?" That was Mr. Buckley again.

This time around, Lisa smiled. I didn't know who Collins was, but she seemed happy to hear his name.

"We went on a vacation last weekend," Lisa answered.

"Cool!" Mr. Buckley said. "I bet you loved it."

Lisa nodded. "I did."

"If Collins is making you happy, hold onto him. He's got a lot of good things for you."

"Thank you, Mr. Buckley."

"Lisa," I muttered to her. "I'm sorry."

Mr. Buckley was laughing. "You don't have to be sorry for her, Natalie. Lisa is no longer in her past. She is living in the present, and there is nothing to be sorry about."

I didn't want to call the therapist cruel, but he seemed to have said that for real. The meeting was not to make anyone feel broken and sad about the past. It was for them to understand the present and try to build a future.

"Who's going next?" asked Mr. Buckley.

An African American woman raised her hand. Mr. Buckley nodded for her to go ahead.

I wondered what she had to say. The woman appeared rich. I could tell from the designer bag on her lap and diamond necklace around her neck. In fact, she was plump and had smooth skin, which was a sign of someone who was fed well.

"Hello, everyone. I'm Jasmine."

"Hi, Jasmine."

"I work as a lawyer, and I've been on the job for five years."

I said it! The woman *was* well off. What could her story possibly be? Rich people hardly ever had issues. They had the money to make their problems go away.

"I love my job because I have always wanted to be a lawyer, even as a young girl. After I got married, my husband left me and the kids because he thought I was too addicted to my work. I was enraged and came to understand that relationships weren't meant for me. It seemed like the men I liked were not comfortable with how much I made, and it affected their pride. So, I decided to stay out of relationships."

So far, so good; her story had nothing horrifying in it. Maybe she was only a woman battling with affairs.

"I have two children, a boy and a girl. The boy's name is Amir, and the girl is Nina. Don't get me wrong, I love my kids more than my job. I mean, it's not like my case files are going to give me grandchildren."

The others laughed at that. I managed a smile. I was eager to get to the part where I would gasp in disbelief.

"When Amir was six and Nina was four, I hired a nanny to take care of them. Her name was Leslie. She was the perfect person for the job. In fact, I felt at ease, knowing I had a competent woman watching over my kids."

Just like Lisa, Jasmine took a long pause. No one had to tell me that she was about to get to the part that brought her to the meeting.

"That was until I saw the scar on Amir's back. I decided to give him a bath one night because he wouldn't stop crying. It seemed like someone had pressed a hot object to his back. When I asked the nanny, she promptly denied. I thought Amir had gotten it from school and reported it to his teacher. She promised to find out who had done it to him. For two months, I didn't know who had hurt my son. Amir wouldn't tell me, but I could see that he was scared. On another night, I was bathing Nina when she complained about her stomach. She collapsed, and I rushed her to the hospital. There, the doctors found the plastic cap of a bottle inside her stomach."

God! These people have been through hell a million times and back. Someone had hurt Jasmine's children! What a demon!

"I thought she swallowed it by mistake or did it intentionally. Whatever it was, Nina didn't know what she was doing. Then three days later, Nina's left eye got swollen. Maybe she had hit her head against something; I wasn't sure."

It *had* to be the nanny. Who else was taking care of the kids and would have had a chance to hurt them? They had found no culprit at the school. Jasmine's problem was in her home!

"That was when I began to have suspicions about my nanny. Nina had to stay home because of the stomach upset she had. My kids hardly played rough, and it couldn't have been anyone from the school because Nina was at home for three days. I asked her again, and she denied any of it. Not convinced by what she said, I walked into a tech store and bought some video cameras. I made sure to install them in her absence and connected the recording to my laptop at the office. For two days, I watched her take care of my kids and nothing suspicious happened. Watching her behave like I would have done to my kids, I felt sorry for suspecting her. I was going to remove the cameras on the third day when it happened."

I leaned forward in my seat, listening with rapt attention. This was it! The woman was about to tell us what the evil nanny had done to her children.

"A man came into the house. From what I could see, the nanny knew him because she kissed him. She had never told me about her boyfriend. I didn't even know she had one. Well, I didn't see anything bad in her trying to meet her lover in my house. But the crazy thing was when they began to have sex in front of my kids!"

"Holy fu…" I began to say but restrained myself.

Mr. Buckley shot me a look, and I muttered an apology to him.

"What was your reaction, Jasmine?" asked the therapist.

"I couldn't believe it. It was disgusting and sickening at the same time. I called my neighbor to knock on my door and stop the madness, but he was in another city. I called the house too, but the nanny ignored my calls. They were forcing my kids to watch them make love. It didn't appear to be the first time. While in the middle of it, Nina began to cry. The nanny walked up to her and slapped her across the face. It caused Amir to reach for his crying sister, but then she yanked him by the hair and pushed him to the floor, away from his sister. There was no way I was going to keep watching that. I called the cops, and they arrested her, but her psychotic boyfriend had vanished."

So, this story wasn't about Jasmine. It was about her kids. There was no way her children's mental health would be the same after going through that. I felt sorry for them.

"How are you kids now, Jasmine?"

A sad smile was on the rich woman's face. "The court took them away from me and handed them to some foster parents. They said I wasn't responsible enough to take care of them."

"And how do you feel about that?"

"I want Amir and Nina back. They are my world, and I would never repeat such a mistake ever again!"

Jasmine had yet to get back her kids. I could almost feel her pain, going home every day to an empty house and remembering her kids were no longer with her. Would those kids hate her? She had brought the nanny into their lives. Would they blame her for their misery?

"What steps are you taking in convincing the court that you're ready to take care of your children again?"

Jasmine thought about this. "I'm planning to quit my job and take up writing. That way, I could always be at home with them."

"You know that the criteria for having your kids with you is being able to financially provide for them, right? How is writing going to help you?"

"A friend of mine has a freelancing website where writers get paid a lot. I think it's going to work out."

Mr. Buckley smiled. "I am happy to hear that. Who's speaking next?"

Before anyone could reply, I raised my hand. Mr. Buckley's smile grew wider.

"Yes, Natalie?"

I cleared my throat and prepared to talk. It was about time these people knew my story.

Day
107
One Hundred Seven

The doorbell rang just as I was stepping out of the shower.

Caleb had gone out and said he wouldn't be back until late. Who could it be? I wasn't expecting anyone. The detective would never dare come to Caleb's place because he knew he would be risking my life if he did so. Lauren had vowed not to visit me until I got the hell out of the house. It couldn't be my parents, either. My mother hated Caleb while my father was still indifferent.

"Who is it?" I called as I got to the door, a towel wrapped around my body.

"It's Lauren," a voice replied.

I was relieved to hear her voice, and at the same time, surprised that she had come to see me. With a big smile on my face, I opened the door.

Of course, it was really Lauren, but she had a pair of sunglasses on her face. Her hair was roughly packed, and her clothes appeared very rumpled. The only other time I had seen Lauren looking like this was when she got depressed.

"Hey, Lauren, come in."

My best friend didn't answer. Instead, she remained where she was, probably staring at me behind those glasses.

"Lauren? Come inside," I said again.

"No," she simply said.

I didn't understand why she refused to step into the place. If she had come all the way from her place to Caleb's house without bothering to call me, then it meant she had something really important to tell me.

I sighed. "He's not at home. Just come inside."

"I…" Lauren stuttered. "I have to tell you something."

The way she acted nervous made me suspect that Lauren was about to confess what Caleb had meant by Pink Alley. It was time she did. Although I wasn't overly bothered about it, I still wanted to know.

"Okay, what's that?"

"Go get dressed. I'll show you."

"Seriously? You're not coming in?"

Lauren shook her head. "No."

I knew that I couldn't change her mind. So, I went back inside, got into some clean clothes, and came back to her. She was already standing beside a yellow convertible.

"Is this yours?" I asked.

Lauren was jiggling the keys in her hand. "It belongs to a friend. He let me borrow it. Come on. You have to see this."

When we got inside the car, and Lauren began to drive out of the parking space, I asked her if it was about Pink Alley. The girl replied in the negative and decided to change the subject.

"How far have you gone with the detective?"

I thought about telling her that she had deliberately changed the topic but felt it wasn't necessary. Lauren had her secrets. Maybe I shouldn't try to poke my nose in them.

"We talked to Cole. He told us a lot of things."

"Really? He finally talked to you about Caleb?"

"Yes," I responded.

"Tell me all about it!"

"Not until you tell me where we are going."

Her excitement vanished. "You'll soon see."

After a few minutes of driving, Lauren turned onto a particular street that I knew was the heart of the city. It was the most populous area in the state, and I could tell that from the number of people who walked down the street. The only times I came here was to use the library and buy my favorite ice cream from one of the kiosks lining the road. Why was Lauren bringing me here?

"Are we going to the library?"

She didn't answer but drove into an alley and parked the car there. It was an illegal parking job, but I knew it would take the patrol cops several hours to notice the car and write us a ticket.

"Get down," Lauren ordered.

I was starting to get scared now. My best friend was acting strange. Why else would she bring me to an alley and ask me to get down behind the car?

I didn't object and did as she said. Lauren began to lead me to one of the many doors on both walls of the alley. There was a particular door with the name – Dark Diner.

She was bringing me to a diner? If Lauren wanted us to eat, then why'd she drive past several delicious places on our way here? What was so special about this place?

Then it hit me again. We were in an alley, and Lauren had a secret about some Pink Alley. What if

Caleb had been talking about this place? But it made no sense. Why were we going into a diner?

Lauren knocked on the door three times before someone answered it. A fat man's face appeared, his gaze falling on me. He broke into a frown as soon as he saw me.

"I brought a friend along," replied Lauren.

The man seemed to consider that and let us in. I found myself in a stuffy kitchen with a lot of cooks moving around and trying not to get behind on their many orders. Maybe Lauren wanted me to see what the kitchen of a diner looked like.

"You want to go down?" the fat man asked.

A sweat dropped from my forehead. The heat was starting to make me feel uncomfortable. If I stayed here another minute, my skin might melt.

"Yes," Lauren answered.

It was now the fat man's turn to lead us. He stopped in front of a door and opened it. What welcomed me was both surprising and confusing.

I could hear music booming from somewhere beneath the building. A staircase led to the basement of the diner. Lauren started to descend down it, and I had no choice but to follow her.

That was when I saw it. There was another world under the restaurant, a world of music, sex, and alcohol. It was like we had stepped into a wild high school party. The sound threatened to damage my eardrums. I didn't know why Lauren had brought me to a club house.

The answer came too soon. Gleaming for everyone to see in pink neon lights was the name Pink Alley. So, Pink Alley wasn't an actual alley. It was a strip club.

There were a lot of people in the club. From men who gawked at the naked strippers on stage to the half-dressed waiters who served them drinks. It was a weird place to be in. I never thought I'd come to a place like this. Now, Lauren had brought me to one.

Honestly, I was trying to get out of a relationship, not get into another one or get laid. How was she not seeing that?

"What is this place, Lauren?" I shouted to her over the loud music.

"Pink Alley!" she called back.

"I know, but why did you bring me here?"

Lauren pulled me to an empty booth in the club where the music was conveniently low. I stroked my ears and hoped I hadn't gone deaf.

"You're not used to the noise," Lauren pointed out.

"Hell, yeah. You know that."

"I just wanted to show you where I work."

Maybe I *had* actually gone deaf and didn't hear her correctly. Did Lauren just say she worked here? How was that even possible?

"Work?"

"Yes, Natalie. I'm a waiter."

Impossible! Lauren would never bring herself to do something like this. I knew we had both talked about getting jobs outside of school, but I would've never thought she'd want to serve drinks to lewd men while being half-naked.

"I don't understand," I said to her.

"This is what I do when I'm not in school. Caleb found out about it and used it to blackmail me. That way, I wouldn't tell everyone at my birthday party that he hits you. I don't know how he found out, but I can't let him tell everyone my secret. After you kept asking me what Pink Alley meant, I felt guilty that you had no idea."

"But…but you're a Christian."

Lauren scoffed. "Of course, I go to church and tried to convert you, but that's because your life is way worse than mine. Do you know how much I get paid just by waiting tables? I have enough money to head off to the Caribbean Islands and spend months there, just sipping coconut water."

I still found it really uncomfortable that my best friend worked here. However, I was glad that she had decided to tell me the truth. She was out to make money. Maybe I shouldn't judge her.

"You don't hate me now, do you?" Lauren decided to ask.

I shook my head. She *was* my best friend. Why would I hate her?

"Detective Lawrence said he wants to bring up a case against Caleb. You don't need to tell everyone what he has been doing to me. You can always just tell the court."

Lauren broke into a smile coated with joy. "Thank God, Natalie, that you're finally going to put that bastard in jail. He has to pay for everything."

I nodded. "Yes, but there's one thing."

Lauren frowned. "What's that?"

"I'm afraid Caleb knows that I'm planning something."

Day
115
One Hundred Fifteen

The smell of fried chicken welcomed me as I walked into the dimly lit room.

I didn't know why the lights were off, but someone was definitely cooking in the kitchen. Was it Caleb? He had talked about not coming home until 10pm. How was he in the kitchen at six, frying chicken and reminding me of how hungry I was?

"Caleb," I called his name, heading toward the aroma.

Of course, he was there, standing beside the stove and turning the meat on a pan.

When he saw me, Caleb broke into a warm smile.

"You're back. I made dinner."

His attitude seemed very weird. Just three days ago, I was telling Lauren about my suspicion. If Caleb knew anything about what I was doing behind his back, he wouldn't be cooking dinner. His hands, I was sure, wouldn't be gripping the stirring fork but my neck. There would be no sound of my stomach rumbling to the tantalizing smell of his meal, but my body writhing from the pain of his actions.

None of that was happening. Caleb was behaving like the nicest man in the world right now. If anyone who had no idea of what he truly did to me walked into the kitchen, they would think my life was perfect, that I didn't have any cause to bury my face in my pillow and cry.

Maybe this was all a trick. Caleb McCord was clever. What if he was waiting for me to confess, playing the good guy so that my heart would get overwhelmed with guilt? I didn't want to think of that. I was doing the right thing. Caleb would never hurt any girl again.

"Why are you home?" I asked him.

Caleb stopped looking at me and turned back to the chicken. He was putting on a dirty apron that I had not bothered to wash for days. The brown shirt he wore under was sleeveless, revealing his strong arms.

His physique was one of the things that made me fall in love with him. At the same time, it was the reason I dreaded him. He could pin me down with one arm and dish out blows with the other. I had no power against him.

"I just got bored of hanging out with my friends," Caleb answered.

That was also strange. Caleb never missed his time out with his friends. I hadn't really met any of them, except Cole.

"Really?" I wanted him to tell me the truth.

He looked at me, his eyes gleaming with such mystery that I pondered on what he had running through his mind. All of a sudden, his food didn't appear enticing anymore. What if he had poisoned it, and today would be the day I die? I could almost picture Caleb standing over my quivering body as I gagged and tried to spit out the poison.

"It's too late, Natalie," he would say. "There's no need to fight it. You have to die now. I know you have been talking to Detective Lawrence."

My world would grow dark right before me, and I would die, drawing my last breath.

"Natalie?" Caleb was calling me. "Are you okay?"

I realized that he must have been talking to me, and I zoned out. My mind had imagined poison that was waiting for me in the fleshy lap of the chicken.

"I'm fine," I answered. "I'm going upstairs to take a shower."

Caleb gave me another warm smile. "Good. You need to freshen up."

While I was in the shower, I thought about calling Lauren. Maybe I should sleep at her place tonight. I didn't trust this kind side of Caleb.

Just last night, around 2am, I woke up to find him staring at me. His look was hard to read because we had turned off the light. But I could feel his eyes on me.

"What are you doing?" I had asked.

Caleb just sighed and went back to sleep. We didn't talk about the weird incident. He eventually went back to sleep, but I couldn't. Why had Caleb been watching me sleep? Was he already contemplating on strangling me?

"The food is going to get cold."

I gasped and dropped the soap. Caleb's voice had startled me. I didn't even hear him walk into the bathroom.

My fiancé was studying my naked body, a lustful look etched on his face. If Caleb had anything on his mind, it was something that I guessed I knew.

"I didn't hear you come in." That was the first thing I said to him.

"Of course, you wouldn't have heard me," Caleb responded. He pointed to the shower. "It's running."

I chuckled nervously, "Yes, it is."

Caleb inched closer, not minding that the shower would make him wet. He pushed me against the wall, and I didn't complain. Although I let out a sound when I almost slipped.

He caught me and didn't mutter any apology. I felt him so close that I wondered what my fate would be today. Was he about to hit me or kiss me? I was naked. The blows would hurt that much more, and I didn't want to fall and get a concussion. At the same time, any kiss from him would set my insides on fire, sheer pleasure vibrating even at the tips of his fingers.

As Caleb pressed me against the wall, my soapy hair dripping onto his clothes, he placed his lips on mine, groping my breasts at the same time.

Damn! How wonderful I felt! How wonderful this beast made me feel!

Caleb's mouth continued to take me in, so much that I turned breathless. My body responded to his love, every part of me screaming his name even as my tongue got lost in his mouth.

However, I soon realized that my breathlessness didn't come from the kiss. It was because Caleb had his hand wrapped around my neck. As his kiss deepened, so did his grip. All of a sudden, the passion turned into one of near death before my eyes. He was choking me, but I wasn't sure he had any idea.

I tried to push him away, but he was strong. My vision spurred while my lips burned. The man before me was crushing my windpipe.

It was when I began to scratch him that he pulled away. Caleb was surprised. Then he saw me cough just as I folded in the waist and drew in air.

"Natalie," he muttered softly. "I'm sorry."

After I was sure that I could breathe, I look up at him. Caleb's clothes were wet, but his face was the same, too. Tears were streaming down his face.

"Oh, god," Caleb exclaimed. "I don't know why I did that."

Absurd, right? Because the next thing I said bore every trace of absurdity.

"No, no," I told him. "You didn't mean to. Don't worry about it."

"I'm never going to do that again."

I nodded. "You should change and wait for me. I'll be with you shortly."

He didn't say anything and walked away. I continued to take my shower. Whenever I washed my neck, the touch hurt me. It wasn't until I stood in front of the mirror to apply some cream on my face that I saw the bruises. Caleb's handprints were on my neck, turning the area red. It was as though he had put his hand in burning coal and seared the prints into my skin.

I thought about taking a picture and sending it to the detective. It was enough evidence that Caleb had hurt me. But I thought about the circumstances of the action. He was kissing me, revealing how much he wanted me while I showered and stood naked before him. Caleb said he didn't mean to, and I believed him. I shouldn't send this to the detective. I couldn't do that to him.

When I walked in to the dining room, Caleb was pouring wine into two glass cups. He saw me and smiled sadly.

"How's your neck?"

"It's no big deal."

I had applied some foundation to hide the mark. But I guessed it didn't work. Caleb could still see it. He brushed a thumb on the mark.

"I'm going to put some…"

I interrupted him. "Come on. It's okay."

We settled down to eat. Caleb had prepared fried rice, fried chicken, potato chips mixed with chicken sauce, and an egg omelet. It wasn't my favorite food but his. Yet, I didn't point it out. If Caleb had taken it upon himself to cook, then he was in a good mood.

As we ate, Caleb told me to tell him about my day. There wasn't much to tell him. I had left for campus around eight in the morning and stayed at the library until it was noon. After that, I met Lauren for lunch and went for Buckley's session by three.

Of course, I skipped that last part. My conversation with Buckley had been about Caleb, as usual. I also told the therapist about my fear that Caleb was plotting something against me.

"It's normal, Natalie, that you feel this way," Mr. Buckley had said. "He has shown you how dangerous he can be. Every act of his seems like a plan to kill or destroy you."

I shook my head. "No. This feels different. He's out to do something, and I don't know what it is."

Buckley just smiled. "You'll be fine, but if you really sense something evil, I'll advise you to go back to your parents' home or back to Lauren's."

I thought about it. "Maybe. I plan to do that tomorrow morning. I'll leave and never return. He's definitely going to call and try to win me back. But I won't listen this time around. I'm done."

But as I ate the delicious meal that Caleb had prepared and saw him smiling happily at me, I wondered if I had the stomach to leave him. Was I really done with Caleb?

"Lauren told you about Pink Alley, didn't she?" Caleb asked me.

I didn't know how to answer him. Lauren had told me not to tell him. She wanted Caleb to believe he still had a hand over her. My best friend had come to accept her job. She wasn't ashamed of it anymore, which meant that Caleb's blackmail wouldn't work.

"No."

Caleb seemed satisfy with my answer, or maybe I was the only one feeling that way. He changed the topic.

"Natalie," started my fiancé. "You love me, don't you?"

I peered into his captivating eyes. I studied his striking looks and remembered that I had fallen for this exact man. That love was long dead. Ever since I met Mandy, I began to understand that my love for him shouldn't exist. I had doused out the flame of our love with my hands by talking to the detective and asking for Buckley's help. If Caleb hadn't sensed it, the best thing was to tell him.

However, I doubted he would take the news calmly. Caleb was a possessive man who wanted to be told that he had not lost his control over someone. People like him would see it as an insult that they no longer had a say in someone else's life. Anytime Caleb got his ego bruised, he lashed out at me.

"Yes, I do," came the lie.

He didn't say anything again, and we ate in silence. After we were done with dinner, I volunteered to clean the dishes. As I was doing that, Caleb snuck up behind me. This was the second time he scared me tonight. He laughed when I dropped the plate in the sink and slightly trembled.

"Why are you scared?" he asked. "There's no one else here but me."

"Shit, Caleb," I responded. "You come up quietly."

"That's the trick," he told me, leaning on the counter.

I continued to wash the plates while he looked at me. After a while, Caleb cleared his throat and spoke,

"You know, we haven't had sex in a long time."

His words surprised me. That wasn't my fault, to be honest. Anytime we came close to having sex, Caleb would pull away and leave the house. It got to a point that I felt he was punishing me. He wanted me to yearn for him, and to be honest, I did.

"I don't...don't know," I replied, stammering.

He grinned. "We can always do that now."

I stared incredulously at him. "Seriously? You want it now?"

Caleb nodded. "Don't you want to?"

"It depends on you, Caleb," I said to him. "Most of the time, I want to sleep with you, but you cut it short. Then you walk away with no explanation."

Caleb sighed. But I thought I saw him grit his teeth at the same time.

"I'm truly sorry for doing that."

Not only did Caleb hurt me physically, he hurt me emotionally, too. It was like he had walked solely into my life just to cause me pain.

"I'm going to make it up to you," he said, and I didn't know what he meant by that until I entered the room minutes later.

Caleb had laid his body out on the bed, wearing nothing but tight boxers that revealed his muscular legs.

He was waiting for me. This was obviously seduction, and I couldn't resist. Soft jazz played from the Bluetooth speaker he had set on my drawer. Making love with that sort of music filtering into my ears always made me feel like I was in Heaven.

"Caleb," I breathed.

"You're still not getting in bed with me after all this?"

I thought he was angry, but honestly, he wasn't. Caleb's grin was evidently plastered on his face. His eyes seductively sized me up.

When he came to me, Caleb kissed me again, this time around, biting my lips gently as he broke the kiss.

"I want you, Natalie," he whispered into my ear. "I hope you do, too."

How in the world wouldn't I? We hadn't even started having sex, and I could almost feel my body melting. His touch, his voice, his fingers trailing my body, transported me into a realm of absolute delight.

I didn't even know when I started to cry. My body quivered from the realization that I missed him! I wished this was the normal life I had with Caleb.

"Yes, Caleb," I told him. "I want you, too."

Then he took me to bed with him.

Day
116
One Hundred Sixteen

The next day, Caleb took me to the boutique. I didn't ask him to, but when I woke up beside him that morning, he kissed my forehead and asked if I would like a wardrobe change.

"That's…" I couldn't find the right words to say. "I'm…"

"I'll take that as a yes," Caleb said and got out of bed.

As I got into the shower, I couldn't stop thinking about last night. If only Caleb could be like that every day. But I was no fool. Something was up, and

I was going to get to the root of it. Whatever Caleb had in store for me, I would find out before he got the chance to do it.

I put on a pair of blue jeans, a white cropped top, and a blue bucket hat. Caleb rubbed the piercing on my navel while he kissed me at the same time. Last night, he had spent a long time just kissing the stud and making me moan.

"You're so damn beautiful," he commented after he stopped kissing me.

I smiled. "Thanks."

Caleb decided to drive my car. He said that his own car had developed a mechanical fault last night, and he would have to take it for repair later in the evening. But he didn't want to break his promise of taking me to the boutique to buy some new clothes.

I didn't argue with him and got into the truck. It wasn't like my car was in good condition either, but Caleb seemed to be comfortable with it. He hummed to the tunes of the radio as we made our way to the mall.

On a day like this, the mall was always crowded. A lot of people had one or a few things to buy. As for Caleb, he said we had a lot to purchase.

We first stopped at an ice cream shop, and he bought me a medium-sized cup of vanilla ice cream with chocolate syrup. It was relieving to feel the icy taste on my tongue as I ate it. I loved ice cream, and Caleb knew that.

"We could get another one," he suggested.

"Oh, no. I had enough," I said. "The boutique?"

Caleb nodded, arched his arm, and allowed me to slip mine into his before leading me to an exotic boutique in the mall. Aphrodite's Palace. I had heard of the store from my rich friends on campus. It wasn't a place for people like me since I didn't have the money to buy a single piece of fabric from the shop.

But it wasn't a problem for Caleb. He chuckled as I stopped in my tracks in front of the boutique, surprised that we were going in there.

"Caleb, they sell very expensive things," I told him.

"I'm not complaining," Caleb answered.

He was right. My fiancé had suggested that we go shopping. He would definitely take care of the bills.

However, this was something I didn't want to do. Lauren had told me not to depend on him. If Caleb chained me to him emotionally, he was definitely doing that with his money, too.

"He's never going to let you go, and you wouldn't want to go either," Lauren had said to me. "Imagine the guilt you would feel because he bought you things, and the only way you can pay him back is by staying with him. That's how you're going to feel, Natalie. So, stop letting him buy you things."

It was too late now to turn back. I couldn't say no to Caleb as we entered Aphrodite's Palace. There would be no end to his insults and beatings if I told him that I didn't want to do this.

"Welcome, Mr. McCord," a pretty young woman with blonde hair greeted him as we walked inside.

She was dressed in a blue suit and had her hair back. To be honest, I felt a stab of jealousy as Caleb smiled back at her.

"Trisha," he said in his usual sexy tone. "It's nice to see you in charge today."

Trisha's smile remained on her face. "Yeah. Emily had something urgent to deal with."

"Oh," Caleb commented. "Meet my girl, Natalie."

My cheeks flustered as he called me his girl. I wasn't sure how comfortable Caleb was introducing me as his girl to others. That had happened before.

A few weeks back, when we went to the beach, Caleb had called me his friend, and I got pissed off. When we got back home, he made sure to beat the shit out of me because he thought I'd embarrassed him in front of his friends.

Those friends kept changing, though. Every time I was out with Caleb, and we stumbled by one of his friends, he would do a casual introduction as though he didn't want me to talk to them. Another day, it would be a different person completely.

"Nice meeting you, Miss Natalie," Trisha bowed to me.

"You too, Trisha."

Then the beautiful shop attendant took us to where the very expensive clothes were hung. Caleb asked her to do that.

He seemed to know his place around the shop, and it bothered me. Aphrodite's Palace sold only women's clothing. How in the world did Caleb know Trisha and the second attendant, Emily? How was he able to find the store's bathroom without asking for directions?

"Excuse me, Trisha," I said to the attendant as she showed me to a black dinner gown, while Caleb was still in the restroom. "Caleb comes here a lot, doesn't he?"

I caught the nervous stare Trisha gave me, but she soon replaced it with a smile.

"He's only been here once or twice, and he just talked with Emily or me," Trisha replied. "Both times, he wanted to buy something for you but couldn't pick the right one."

I knew she was lying, but I didn't push further. Maybe she wasn't, and my mind only wanted me to believe that Caleb was cheating on me. He could be bringing dozens of girls into Aphrodite's Palace, buying clothes for them, or he could be dating one of the employees. Maybe it was Trisha!

Caleb hardly bought clothes for me. Just jewelry, ice cream, take-out food, shoes, and so many other things Aphrodite's Palace didn't sell. Yet, he was very familiar with the place.

To be honest, I was being unreasonable. What if Caleb knew this place before we started dating or before we ever met? I shouldn't try to judge him because he knew a place that was meant for women.

"Honey," he was back. "Did you find something you like?"

I feigned a smile and pointed at the dinner gown that Trisha had showed me.

"I want this one."

After about thirty minutes of perusing the shop, I was able to pick at least twenty other items, all of which Caleb paid for. During the time I was choosing the clothes, he had struck a conversation with a teenage customer who had a very beautiful face and long black hair parted in the middle. I saw them laughing as though they had known each other for a long time and felt very envious. To be honest, I just wanted to get out of there.

As we walked back to my truck, Caleb helping with most of the bags, I asked him something I shouldn't have asked.

"Do you have to talk to every beautiful girl you meet?"

I thought he was going to flare up and insult me. But Caleb didn't. He just put the bags in the trunk and looked at me.

"I'm sorry if I made you jealous."

That statement took all the anger out of me. I didn't know what to do. In fact, I felt very ashamed for acting like a child. He wasn't flirting. Caleb was just friendly.

"I'm sorry, too," I told him.

My fiancé kissed me on the cheek. "Let's not talk about it again."

He got behind the wheel and waited for me to get inside. Somehow, as I fastened my seatbelt, and he backed out of the mall's parking lot, I felt Caleb's impatience. He kept tapping his fingers on the steering wheel and exceeded the speed limit a little bit. Was it because of what I said to him? Was he eager to get out of the truck and away from me?

I decided not to say anything and texted Lauren instead. She didn't respond, but I left her a message saying that I would make my escape tomorrow morning. Today was meant to be the day I finally leave Caleb, but we had fucked last night. It ruined my plan, but there will always be another day.

"You should put your phone away," Caleb's voice came.

I glanced sideways at him. "Why?"

"There is something I want to show you."

It took me a few seconds to realize that we weren't on the way back home. Instead, Caleb had taken us down another route, toward the campus.

"Where are we going?" I asked.

Caleb smiled a little. "Just put the phone in the glove compartment."

I gripped my phone in my hand. "And why should I do that?"

I saw his hand stiffen as he held onto the steering wheel. Caleb was starting to get angry, but he wore his smile.

"Don't you trust me?"

"I do, but where are we going?"

Caleb sighed and replied. "To meet my father."

That caught me off guard. His father? Caleb knew where his father was? The news had been that the senator vanished, and no one knew where he was. Either Caleb was lying or hallucinating, or he indeed knew where his father was because he had kidnapped him!

"What do you mean by your father?"

"Several years ago, he suffered a heart attack," Caleb explained. "The doctors said he would never be able to walk again. It also affected his brain, and he couldn't remember anything or anyone. I figured out it would be best to keep him somewhere safe, away from the media who would never stop talking about his illness and ruin his reputation. I bought a house for him and have been keeping him there."

I didn't want to believe Caleb, but maybe he was telling the truth. On a few occasions, I had found drug prescriptions in his drawer but thought he was probably using them for himself. Now, it made more sense to me. Those drugs were meant for a really sick person. Caleb was really taking care of his father.

"So, what's wrong with my phone?" I asked.

"I don't want you telling anyone about it, not even Lauren," he said and begged me with his eyes. "The only way I can trust you is if you keep it in the glove compartment."

"Fine," I responded and did as he said. "Happy now?"

Caleb beamed at me. "Thank you."

The house Caleb got for his father was located in the far area of the city. It had a black gate guarded by a bald man who waved happily at Caleb when he saw us in the car.

After that, we drove along a wide road that led us to the front porch of an old building that looked very much like a British castle.

We were welcomed by an old woman in white maid clothes who took my bag and asked if I wanted a cup of tea. For a brief moment, I thought that I was, somehow, part of royalty.

"Her name is Denise," Caleb said to me as I told the woman that I would tell her later if I wanted a cup of tea or not.

"She's a maid?" I asked Caleb.

He was leading me into the house now. "Not just a maid, but my father's favorite employee. She has been with our family for two decades now."

"Wow, she must really like this family."

It was good to know that I could ask someone else about Caleb's life. Cole Watkins had told me that my fiancé came from a troubled home, but I wanted to hear it from someone else. I wanted to know if it was true, what he had said about Caleb.

When we got into the house, Caleb took me to the back veranda where he was sure his father would be. As part of his therapy, the doctors had instructed Caleb to take his father outside once in a while. On the back veranda, he could stare at the grassy land of the mansion, watch the butterflies perch on beautiful flowers growing on them. I didn't know how Caleb had gotten enough money to buy a vast land such as this. Maybe he took out his father's money.

Indeed, we met Mr. McCord there. He was in a wheelchair, lost in the beauty of the land before him.

It wasn't until I got to see his face that I realized how pathetic his situation was. A man like Mr. McCord wasn't lost in the beauty of any place. I doubt he had any idea what he was seeing or where he was.

Mr. McCord was an old man with grey hair. Caleb looked very much like him, except for the color of his eyes. They were shockingly glassy as though he was blind. I could see wrinkles lining up on every part of his body, turning him into a really old man. His head was bent to one side while both of his hands were curled up, unmoving. It looked more like the man had suffered a stroke and not a heart attack.

"Dad," Caleb crouched in front of him. "It's me, your son. I brought Natalie here, just like you asked me to."

Day
118
One Hundred Eighteen

The second dream came around three in the morning. I refused to sleep on the bed, having crawled into the empty wardrobe and crying my eyes out.

Having lost the strength to cry further, I gave in to sleep. The first dream wasn't one I could vividly remember, but I knew that Caleb was chasing me with a baseball bat, and my leg got caught in a mouse trap. As the cry of agony escaped my lips, Caleb got to me. He swung the bat once, and I woke up.

I was still in the wardrobe, and it was very dark. The smell of old wood clogged my nose, but that didn't deter me from falling asleep.

I was soon back in the dreamland where I came across Caleb's father.

He was in the middle of the road, standing on both feet. Mr. McCord's tears were of blood, frightening me to the bones.

"You shouldn't have believed him," he said. "My son is a monster."

But it wasn't his voice I heard. It was Caleb's voice.

"Please, how can I save myself?" I yelled.

Before Mr. McCord could answer, a bus appeared out of nowhere and ran him over. I screamed as I heard the sound of bones crushing, and his brain dropping on the concrete.

Driving the bus was Caleb. He had a wicked grin on his face as he stepped down from the bus. A baseball bat was in his hand, dripping blood. It was as though I was looking at the face of Satan himself.

"Run, Natalie, but I'll always be ahead of you!"

I couldn't even move. Somehow, I was rooted to a spot. When I looked at my feet, one of them was caught in a mouse trap again. A shadow towered over me, and it turned out to be Caleb, bringing down the bat to my head.

I woke up again. By this time, it was morning. I could tell by the bright light seeping through the doors of the wardrobe where I had not fully shut it.

I wanted to stay in there all day, not minding the weakness that overpowered me and the sound of my stomach rumbling. I hadn't touched my food in days. If I stayed here, I would die. But it was okay. I wanted to die. I wanted this pain to end.

Just then, I heard someone enter the room. I pressed my back against the wall of the wardrobe, hoping the person would have no idea I was there.

But that didn't happen. In no time, I heard the wardrobe creaking open just as the full glare of the lit room burst into my vision. I blocked my eyes with my hand, wincing in pain.

"Miss Natalie," I heard Denise, the maid's voice. "It's time to eat."

"Leave me alone," I told her weakly.

"No, I can't," Denise answered. "You haven't eaten in two days."

"Just let me be."

"Mr. McCord won't allow that. You have to eat."

For a brief moment, I thought she cared about me. but that wasn't true. Denise was only following orders. It was the order of her master, Caleb McCord.

"I don't want to eat your fucking food!" I said with the little strength I had.

Denise sighed and backed away from the wardrobe. "You leave me no choice. Boys!"

Just as she said that, two men stepped into the room and headed for where I was hiding. I knew what they were about to do.

"No, no, no," I began to protest, but they were much stronger than I was.

The men pulled me out of my hiding place and carried me to the bed. There, they pinned me to the white sheets just as Denise tried to force food into my mouth.

I keep spitting it out and gritted my teeth so she wouldn't have access. Denise was clearly frustrated. She dropped the spoon angrily and brought out a small bag. The men were still holding me down.

"I really don't want to do this, but Mr. McCord wants you to eat," she said. "You're not going to die on my watch."

"Burn in hell!"

Denise ignored me as she pulled a syringe out of her back pocket. I started fighting again as I saw her draw clear liquid from a bottle, kicking and hoping to free myself.

"What are you doing?" I cried.

"What is necessary," Denise responded. "Please, hold her down."

I couldn't even move from how much I was pinned down by the two men. Denise found a vein in my arm and inserted the needle, filling me with whatever was in the bottle. Tears poured from my eyes as she did so.

"See," she said. "It wasn't that bad. You can let her go."

Just as I felt the men's hands leave my body, I sat up straight, hoping to punch Denise in the nose. However, a strong force pushed my body back. It wasn't the men this time around. It was my own body.

All of a sudden, I was weaker, mind spinning as I tried to fight whatever was happening to me. I couldn't even feel my fingers or my legs or the bed I was supposedly lying on.

"What did you do to me?" I asked, but it was like my lips refused to move.

Denise's face was over me. Her smile comforting.

"Would you like to eat now, Miss Natalie?"

The aching pain in my belly had intensified. In fact, it was as though someone was squeezing my intestines.

"Yes, please," those words came out of me.

Two days ago

Caleb McCord's plan had not been to take me to see his father. It was a perfect plan to abduct me.

Of course, everything he said about the house was real. The man in the wheelchair was actually his father. He was truly taking care of the man. The only thing he failed to tell me was that I would never be returning home.

"You have to stay here," he said to me on the day we arrived at the house.

"What do you mean?" I thought he was joking.

"You have new clothes from the boutique, and I can get you more," Caleb responded. "But you have to stay here."

"What? That's ridiculous!" I said, laughing. "This is your father's house. Why do I have to stay here?"

"Because I said so!" That was when his expression changed.

Caleb had unleashed the beast out of him. His eyes burned with fury, so much that I had to take a step back in fright.

"My phone," I stammered. "I have to tell someone if you're going to make me stay here."

Caleb clenched his fist. "Are you deaf? You're staying here and not telling anyone about it."

That was when it hit me! Caleb had kidnapped me. He had made me leave my phone in the car so that I wouldn't have access to it.

Tears flowed down my cheeks as I asked, "Why are you doing this?"

He unclenched his fist and walked over to the table in the room, pouring himself a glass of water.

"Because you're trying to run away from me," he said. "I don't want you to run from me."

"But I'm not," I told him. "I'm right here with you, Caleb."

"Stop lying to me!" Caleb yelled and threw the glass cup in his hand against the wall, causing it to shatter and the shards to fall on the rug.

I hoped Denise or one of the guards had heard this. Maybe they would come to save me. I kept staring at the door leading out of the room, expecting one of them to burst through and save my life.

Caleb must have seen me look at the door. "No one is coming to save you, Natalie."

"What?"

"They work for me," he said, rubbing his knuckles and walking toward me. "They know you're not to leave this house."

My back was now against the wall. I heaved with tears, thinking about how to beg Caleb to let me go.

Maybe if I assured him that I would never leave him, he would change his mind.

"Caleb, I love you," I said to him. "You don't have to do this."

"You're a liar, Natalie," my fiancé said and grabbed me by the neck, almost crushing my windpipe.

"No, please," I tried to say, but his grip was causing me to lose air.

In addition to that, Caleb began to pound my head against the wall, so that I felt the strong need for oxygen and pain in my scalp at the same time.

"You fucking liar!" he said and finally let go of me.

I slid to the floor, holding my neck and crying like a child. Caleb just watched me.

"When were you going to tell me the truth?" he demanded.

"What truth?" I quickly replied. "I have never lied to you."

Without warning, Caleb kicked me in the thigh. I yelped as a sharp pain tore up my leg. He proceeded to kick me several times until I was shielding myself with my arms and letting them get the brute of the blows.

"When were you going to tell me about Buckley's?"

Oh my god! Caleb indeed knew about the therapy. I had my suspicions, and now, it was too late for me as I realized that the suspicion was right.

"I'm sorry," I replied, whimpering. "I was… going to tell you."

"You bitch!"

The kicks had now turned into punches. Caleb grabbed me by the hair and pushed me to the center of the room. I cried helplessly as his blows connected with my jaw and ribcage. Caleb was hurting me!

"I'm sorry," I kept begging.

His guards and Denise were definitely as heartless as he was. Why didn't they come to save me? Even if Caleb had ordered them not to react, were my cries of pain not enough to make them disobey the order?

"What about Detective Lawrence?" Caleb said again. "Do you think I'm that dumb?"

By now, he had stopped beating me. I crawled away from him, spitting blood onto the rug. One of my eyes was so swollen that I couldn't see clearly.

"Tell me about Detective Lawrence," Caleb said behind me. "What have you told him?"

I shook my head. "Nothing. I told him nothing."

Caleb scoffed. "I don't believe you. That's why you have to stay here. Don't worry; no one is going to look for you. I'll make sure of that."

Then he left the room. For at least thirty minutes, I was on the rug, crying at my misfortune. Why was it that every time I got the relief that Caleb had truly changed, it would turn into a lie, one that unexpectedly threw me into a world of misery? When would this stop, all of it?

I heard someone walk inside. I couldn't even raise my head to look at their face, but from the pair of black women shoes that I set my partially blind sight upon, I knew it was Denise.

"I have to treat your wounds," she said to me.

I didn't say anything as she pulled me to my feet and started treating the wounds Caleb had inflicted on me. I realized that she refused to look up at me. Was she feeling guilty for not intervening and letting Caleb turn me into a punching bag?

"I need a phone," I told her. "Can I get a phone? I need to speak to someone."

I was wrong about Denise. When she stared at me, her gaze was so cold that it pierced the hope I had growing in my heart that she would save me.

"Mr. McCord's orders. You're not to talk to anyone."

"But you can't possibly let him do this to me!" I cried.

"It's none of my business."

"Why are you talking to her?" Caleb was back with the bags from the boutique.

Denise immediately rose to her feet, lowering her gaze and apologizing. I could see her hands tremble. The woman was equally afraid of Caleb. Did he beat her, too?

"You're not to talk to her," Caleb bellowed. "She planned to ruin my life."

"I am sorry, Mr. McCord," she apologized again and walked out of the room.

Caleb threw the bags at my feet, spewing the clothes on the rug. I didn't even move a muscle and only watched him with disgust.

"There," Caleb said. "I'll get you more."

"What are you going to tell the detective when he starts looking for me?" I asked him before he could leave the room. "He suspects you already."

Caleb paused at the door for a few seconds before he turned back to look at me. "So, you've actually been telling him a lot of things?"

I grinned, not minding that Caleb could beat me again for what I was about to say.

"Because he needed to know. By the way, I met Mandy. She revealed a lot, too."

Caleb didn't hurt me. Instead, he came to sit beside me, hugging my head.

"What did you learn from Mandy?"

"That your father tried to abduct her, but she got away. It's the same thing you're doing to me, but sadly, your father can't come to your aid, so you have to do it on your own. It's surprising how you have refused to change, Caleb. Always predictable!"

"Mandy would have ruined my father's reputation. He didn't want that. Your situation is very different."

"Lies, Caleb." I laughed. "You never stop telling them."

"Whether you choose to believe me or not," Caleb responded. "I am doing this because I love you. The detective would take you away from me. Also, Buckley. I know of your plans, Natalie. I saw them on your phone."

"So, apart from beating the shit out of me, you've been snooping around on my phone? How low of you, Caleb! How low!"

Caleb just wore this very sad look. "See, you never would have spoken to me that way. You've changed, Natalie, and that's what I'm scared of. I'm afraid you don't love me anymore."

"Yes, Caleb!" I cried. "I don't love you anymore. I can't keep up with your shit anymore or your insanity."

Caleb rose to his feet and made for the door again.

"Denise will show you to your room!"

"You bastard! I don't want to stay here! Fuck you! I wanna go home!"

But he didn't listen to me. I raced after him as he walked out of the house, but his guards soon stopped me. I continued to yell as Caleb drove my truck away, but if he heard me, he didn't act like his ears were working.

As Caleb left me, my cries soon dropped to sobs until the silence of the mansion was all I could hear.

Day
121
One Hundred Twenty-One

For three more days, I stayed in that house. Denise didn't have to plead with me to eat. Whatever she had in the syringe did the magic.

However, because I didn't want to be controlled by some drug and wanted to have a clear mind when thinking of how to escape, I decided not to starve myself. I would play Caleb and Denise's little game.

But I soon realized it was impossible to escape from that house. Once, I had stumbled on an old wire phone, but it wasn't working. I snuck it into my room and spent hours on it, trying to make it work. It didn't.

Another time, I stole Denise's phone, but it was also pointless. For some odd reason, the house had no signal. I couldn't even send a text message.

The guards watched the place 24/7. If I walked into the bathroom and peered through the window, they were always everywhere. The windows were sealed shut and bulletproof. I couldn't break them even if I tried.

There was no basement either; the hope for a tunnel that would lead to my freedom was crushed. No chimney, either. No place for me to crawl through and be far from this hellhole.

Denise allowed me to watch TV, but I didn't see any news about me missing. Had Caleb been able to convince everyone that I was alright? Had the detective or Buckley believed him? Worse, did something bad happen to them?

"I want to talk to Caleb," I said to Denise one morning as she made breakfast. "I can't continue with this madness."

Denise didn't so much as glance at me. She just continued chopping the onions and humming to herself.

I grabbed her by the arm and forced her to look at me. "Put me through to Caleb, now!"

Denise glared at me. "Didn't you steal my phone the other day? You can't reach anyone here. No signal."

I let go of her arm. "But I need to talk to him! He has to let me go."

"That's not going to happen, Miss Natalie."

I glanced around for something I could use to show how serious I was. My eyes fell on the knives on the plate rack, and I pulled out one of them. Denise raised an eyebrow at me.

"I'm going to kill myself then!" I threatened, although anyone could tell that I was bluffing.

Denise just shrugged. "Go ahead."

"I'm serious, Denise," I continued to bluff. "I'm going to take my own life. I wonder what Caleb is going to do to you. He loves me, and he would hate you for not stopping me."

Denise began to laugh. There was no doubt that she was mocking me.

"Loves you?" she spoke. "Alright, believe that all you want."

I was shocked by her attitude. It was like she knew something that I didn't know.

"What?"

Denise ignored me and began to pour tea into a cup. She placed it on a tray and walked out of the kitchen.

"Answer me, Denise!"

I soon figured out where she was going. Denise was about to serve Mr. McCord his tea. The man was on the veranda, as usual. He was still the helpless man that I first saw, unaware that his son was holding me prisoner.

"I have nothing to tell you," Denise said as she fed Mr. McCord.

I stared at the two of them. For some reason, I felt that Denise cared about Caleb's father a lot. She nurtured him with this caring attitude that was evident.

"Is it true what happened?" I asked Denise.

She didn't answer me. Tea dropped down Mr. McCord's beard, and she immediately wiped it clean.

"Is it true that Caleb's father…?" I didn't know how to say this. "Caleb's father impregnated his own sister, and the result was Caleb?"

That was when Denise reacted to my words, showing me that she had been listening to me talk but refused to respond.

"Where did you hear that nonsense?"

I wasn't going to tell her that I heard it from Cole Watkins. When he told Detective Lawrence and me, we couldn't believe our ears. Caleb was a result of incest? How in the world was that possible?

"Mr. McCord raped his own sister," Cole had said. "We did a DNA test to prove it. I remember Caleb finding out and losing his sanity. It really tore him apart. But the McCord family wanted to keep the secret. They got Mr. McCord a woman who would pretend to be Caleb's mother."

"The flight attendant?" Detective Lawrence had asked.

Cole nodded. "Yes. She knew all about it, but they paid her to keep her mouth shut. Yet, they couldn't hide the truth from Caleb. He considered himself an abomination and tried to kill himself. That was when they brought him to the mental facility. He kept coming back, though. At least, he was sent here twelve times after there were no signs of him recovering. I became his doctor the last time he was here."

"It must have changed him," I said to Cole and the detective. "The truth about himself broke him."

"But it's no justification for what he did to you and Mandy," Detective Lawrence said. "I know anyone who have been traumatized like that is truly broken, but you're also a person that shouldn't be hurt by someone else's misery."

"Caleb is the son of Mr. McCord and his sister. He was born through incest," I told Denise.

"Stop saying that!" She suddenly shouted, rising to her feet and causing the tea to spill on Mr. McCord, who didn't seem to feel anything.

Denise didn't even care that she had burned her boss. She walked toward me, her eyes blazing with rage. There was something familiar about the way she revealed her anger. It was almost as if I had seen it before.

"Don't you ever say that!"

"It's the truth, isn't it?" I continued, sure that I would receive a slap for not shutting up. "Your reaction says it's true. Caleb is an abomination."

That was when Denise squealed and hit me across the face. I staggered backward, holding my cheek.

Denise's gaze was murderous. "You had it coming. I don't appreciate anyone talking about Mr. McCord that way."

I scoffed. "He got it from you, didn't he?"

Denise was back to cleaning Mr. McCord's hand, where she had spilled the tea.

"Got what from me?"

"His temper," I answered.

My cheeks had stopped stinging, maybe because I hadn't realized a greater truth that made me forget a mere maid had hurt me.

"Your words are unclear, Miss Natalie."

"You're his mother, Denise. You're Mr. McCord's sister."

"I don't know what you're talking about." That was Denise's response, but she was not a good liar.

I had seen my answer on her face. The truth dwelled in her eyes.

"Of course, you do," I insisted. "You look at me the same way he does."

Denise had now finished cleaning up Mr. McCord. She packed the teacup and the tray, and made her way to the kitchen again.

"You're not a maid here," I continued, following her. "You're here because Caleb is your son. Did he lock you up here like he's doing to me? How about Mr. McCord? Did he really suffer a heart attack?"

"Girl, don't speak about things you don't know," Denise responded.

"I am sure about this," came my words. "When you are beside Mr. McCord, the resemblance with Caleb is striking. You're his parents."

"So, what if I am? That's not your ticket out of here. You can't blackmail me with it!"

"You're scared of him," I told the woman. "I saw you tremble when he caught you talking to me. If he has you locked up too, we can both work together to save ourselves. Caleb shouldn't be controlling us!"

Denise dropped the tray into the sink and continued to chop the onions from earlier. She didn't want to talk to me, but I decided that my persistence would make her speak.

"Just tell me how to get out of here," I said to her. "I can call for help. I can save us both."

"I love my son," Denise finally confessed. "I don't want to leave him."

"Has he manipulated you, too?" I got close to her and asked. "That you don't know what is right from wrong? This isn't right. Caleb is keeping us as prisoners. We have to set ourselves free."

"You're the only prisoner here," Denise told me. "I came here to take care of my brother."

But it was clear that Denise was also under Caleb's manipulation. I didn't know how Caleb did it, but he seemed to know how to confuse a woman, so that she would do everything he asked of her. He had done it to me several times, and each time, Caleb won.

How was he manipulating Denise? Was he trying to make her suffer for bringing him into this world? Cole had talked about how Caleb hated his true mother. She should have aborted him when she had the chance. He also hated his father. He was the rapist who sired a taboo.

Why was Caleb keeping all of them here? Was this a perfect plan to bring everyone in his life together and torture them? I wondered who he would bring next into this prison of his. Cole Watkins? Would he hunt down Mandy? What about Lauren? Caleb could go after her, too. She knew too much about him!

"Please, Denise," I said to her. "You need to get me out of here!"

"No, she isn't!" Caleb had suddenly appeared in the kitchen.

I squealed like a frightened rabbit when I learned of his presence. How did he keep doing that, appearing without anyone hearing him? Even Denise had gasped in fright. She dropped the knife and stepped away from me.

"And why would she try to rescue you?" Caleb asked, walking toward us.

I stole a glance at Denise, expecting her to say something. Would she tell Caleb that I had learned of his birth? Would she tell her son that I knew everything about him?

"I never said that I would help her," Denise defended herself. "She was begging, but I wasn't going to do it."

Caleb groaned and dropped a bag of groceries onto the kitchen counter. "Whatever. Get me something to eat."

Denise quickly nodded and got to work. I looked from her to Caleb and knew that I wasn't wrong. The boy looked like her a lot, more than he looked like his father. The only problem was that I didn't know why Denise was so scared of him. It was like he had a chain of control around her neck, pulling her like a dog.

"How have you been?" Caleb asked as he sat by the counter.

You would think he cared about me. But he didn't. If Caleb had locked me up in this house so as to protect himself from law enforcement agents, there was absolutely no evidence that he cared about me.

"How's that any of your business?" I asked rudely.

"Oh, come on, Natalie," Caleb said. "What exactly do you want? You complain when I don't care about you. You complain when I do."

"Get me out of this place. That's what I want."

Caleb sighed. "I was thinking about bringing in some games for you. Maybe Scrabble or Chess?"

"You're full of bullshit, Caleb McCord! You're fucking insane," I shouted at him. "Why do you have to punish me for what happened to you?"

Caleb frowned. Then he looked at Denise. "Did you tell her anything?"

The maid shook her head. "I didn't. She found out on her own."

Caleb slammed his fists on the counter and rose to his feet. I thought he was coming for me again, but that didn't seem to be on his mind. He just walked away and said nothing.

"You've made him really angry," Denise told me.

"It's not my problem. You and your son should stop hurting me."

Day

123

One Hundred Twenty-Three

Two days later, Denise decided to talk to me. I had no idea what changed her mind, but maybe like me, she was starting to see that Caleb was truly a monster.

"Hey," she greeted, poking her head into the room.

I was sitting in front of a mirror and brushing my hair. When I heard Denise's voice, I didn't bother replying. She had annoyed me by striking me on the cheek because I talked about her son. But I wasn't wrong. The two of them *were* crazy. Caleb had gotten his rage from this woman.

Ever since Cole told the detective and me about Caleb's true identity, I had gone on to ask if that sort of birth could make someone become a psycho. Cole said no. The only downside to incest was the abnormal effect it would have on later generations. But an immediate offspring would be like every other child.

Denise had no record of insanity, neither did Mr. McCord. Caleb was insane because he had made himself that way. He had dwelled on the way he had been born and decided to turn himself into a beast because of that.

"It's no one's fault that Caleb is that way," Cole said. "It's his fault."

"Can he be cured?" I asked desperately.

"Caleb doesn't want to do that. He sees himself as incurable."

Denise was now inside the room. I could see her approaching from the reflection in the mirror.

"Hey," the woman said again.

"What do you want?" I eventually said to her. "You want to tell me how I can escape from here?"

Denise shook her head. "That's impossible. I don't even know how to do that. The guards won't let me."

I turned to look at her, lowering my voice.

"You're the cook, aren't you? You can always drug their meal or something, and we can get the fuck out of here."

"But what about Mr. Mc…my brother?" Denise asked. "Caleb is going to kill him if he finds out that we escaped."

I frowned. "What do you mean by kill him?"

Denise decided to sit on the bed. She was quivering with tears. I didn't know why she had started to cry, but I didn't pity her. Maybe this was all an act, some plan to manipulate me. I wouldn't be surprised if Caleb was behind this.

"You really don't know what he has done to the man," Denise responded. "My brother wasn't always like this."

I wasn't sure that I understood what she was saying. But Denise was trying to tell me something.

"Caleb said it was a heart attack."

Denise wiped off her tears. "When did you start believing Caleb? Has he ever told you the truth?"

To be honest, I couldn't confidently say Caleb had ever told me the truth, not even once. He was always hiding the truth from me and making me look like a fool.

"It wasn't a heart attack?" I asked.

Denise sniffled. "He shouldn't know that I told you this. But Caleb kidnapped me from my home, the exact way he did to you. He said we were going on a trip. I chose to believe him. But it was a very big lie. Caleb brought me to this house, where I saw my brother wounded. His own son had hurt him."

I gasped. What a horrific revelation! Caleb had crippled his father? He had damaged his brain, too?

"That's…" I said, rising to my feet. "That's terrible."

"I was so scared because Caleb was hell-bent on killing the two of us. He blamed us for his psychological disorder. He said we made him end up at the mental facility. Although I hated my brother for what he did, I couldn't let him die. I had to beg Caleb. I promised that I would take care of his father, and no one would ever have to know what he did."

"That was how you ended up here."

"Yes," Denise replied. "I've been here ever since. You're right, Natalie. I'm a prisoner here, too."

I had vowed not to feel sorry for Denise, but looking at her, there was no way that a normal human wouldn't feel sorry for her. Caleb was an exception. He wasn't normal. That was why he was holding his parents as captives, having ruined the life of his father.

"We need to think of something, Denise," I said to her. "I think fate brought me here for a reason. It's time that you and Mr. McCord leave this prison."

Denise glanced sideways at me. "How do you suppose we do that?"

"I think I might have a plan."

Caleb came back in the evening. He didn't appear drunk, but I could smell beer wafting from his breath.

When he tried to kiss me, I pulled away from him, wondering what had come over him. He just groaned and flopped down on the sofa in the living room.

"Lauren called."

Ah, yes, Caleb had my phone. He had access to all my calls, my text messages, and all my social media chats.

"What did you tell her?"

"Oh, I didn't speak to her," he said and pulled out my phone. "You're going to assure her again that you're really fine."

The day after Caleb abducted me, he came back to the house and made me speak to Lauren. I refused to do what he said at first, but he threatened to beat me up if he didn't.

I wasn't going to let him. My plan was to get out of here in one piece.

So, I took the phone and talked to Lauren, telling her that I was fine and that Caleb and I had gone on vacation. We would be back after a while. Caleb also made me cancel my appointments with Buckley. I relayed the same message of being on vacation with Detective Lawrence. The man didn't seem to believe me, but what else could I say?

Now, here was Caleb again, asking me to speak with Lauren. My best friend was probably worried about me, or she didn't believe the story about the fake vacation.

"Natalie," I heard Lauren say in relief over the phone.

"Hey, Lauren, how are you?"

"I'm good. Are you still with that monster?"

I glanced at Caleb, who was watching me with an intense glare. On his order, I had put the phone on speaker. Caleb clearly heard Lauren call him a monster.

"Yes, I am."

"When are you coming back home?" she asked.

I looked at Caleb again. He mouthed the reply to me.

"Very soon. I don't know yet. I'm really starting to like this place."

"Where exactly are you? Is he making you lie?" Lauren asked me.

"No, Lauren. Caleb wants to change, for real. He took me here so we could spend time together."

"Well, you have to show me pictures so I'm convinced."

I glanced at Caleb again. He rolled his eyes and told me to say yes.

"Of course," I said. "I'll text you."

That was when Denise came into the room. She served Caleb his food. The man glared at her.

"I'm not eating."

"But you told me to make something for you," Denise replied.

Lauren had heard it. "Who is that? And did I just hear Caleb's voice?"

"Oh, it's nothing. It's a friend we have over here. Her name is Denise."

Caleb was signaling to me to cut the call, but I pretended not to see him.

"She is a cook and damn, the food she makes! You should try it some time, Lauren."

Caleb was now at my side. He tried to yank the phone from me, but I moved away. His eyes began to reveal his rage. This was the moment that I was waiting for. I knew that Caleb would not try to harm me, not with Lauren on the phone.

Yet, I needed him to be angry. It was what would work for the plan. Caleb moved closer to me, gesturing that he would crush me with his hands. Denise was behind him. I saw her pull out an object.

"But I don't know where you are," Lauren said.

"It's in a castle, somewhere…"

That was when Caleb slapped my hand, causing the phone to fall. At the same time, Denise made her move. Swiftly, she plunged something into the throbbing vein in Caleb's neck. It was a syringe.

The surprised Caleb fell back, pulling the syringe out of his neck. He couldn't believe that Denise would use his own drug on him. As he tried to attack her, Caleb fell to the ground, unable to move.

I picked the phone off the ground. Lauren hadn't hung up yet.

"Lauren, you need to come and save me!"

Day
129
One Hundred Twenty-Nine

I was sitting in the interrogation room of the police department when Detective Lawrence walked in.

He came in with a bald man of average height, who kept pushing his circle-rimmed glasses up his nose. The detective was happy to see me on my feet.

Ever since Lauren saved me from that prison of Caleb's, I fell ill for a week, possibly because of what I had gone through there.

As for Caleb, the police weren't able to find him. Denise had asked me to lock him in one of the wardrobes. She didn't want her son going to jail, not by her hands.

I objected to that. The truth was, I wanted Caleb to pay for everything, from hurting Mandy to ruining my life. I wanted him to be locked up because of that. His place was in a mental facility, not the sane world where the normal people lived.

However, I understood Denise's plight. She still loved her son and would do anything for him. But her stay in his prison was over. It was time for her and her brother to go home.

"Just leave him here," the woman said to me as we dragged Caleb into the wardrobe. "They'll probably find him here or not. But I'm not going to be the reason my son spends the rest of his life in jail."

So, I told Lauren that he had driven away a few minutes after I asked her to save me. He was probably out there somewhere, not aware that his cell had been infiltrated.

By the time they figured out I was lying, Caleb was already gone. The stupidity of that act of putting him in the wardrobe hit me a few days later.

What if Caleb comes back for me? What if he finds me again and kills me? He was undeniably unstable and would do clearly irrational things.

Two days later, my fear of not knowing where Caleb was came to an end. The cops found him getting gas at a station close to my school. It was scary that they found him there, so close to me. Had Caleb really come after me?

His trial would start in a few days time. There were a lot of evidence against him. When the cops arrested him, Caleb had recordings of everything that went on in that house in his car. It included the time that he had beat me.

His guards agreed to testify against him. The doctor who had treated his father was also one of the testifiers. My mother and Lauren were ready to sit in the box and talk about Caleb's insane acts. I didn't know if Denise would do it. I hadn't heard from her since we got out. Mandy was one of the testifiers, too. In short, Caleb McCord was definitely going to jail.

I was here because the police wanted to know if I would tell the court what Caleb did to me. As much as I wanted to see him behind bars, a part of me still pitied him. Caleb was sick. He needed therapy, not jail.

"Miss Grace," Detective Lawrence said after he introduced the second detective with him as Henry Court. "We are going to start by having your confession on tape."

"Confession?"

"Yeah, the truth about Caleb McCord."

I looked at the detective for a long time. He had placed a tape recorder on the table, expecting me to give him the go ahead to record.

"Ah, Miss Grace, don't tell me you're having second thoughts," said the detective.

I shrugged. "Well, I don't know."

"We talked about this," Detective Lawrence said. "Your testimony is very important to this case. We need you to tell the court why we want Caleb in jail."

"Is there no other penalty for his act besides jail? I mean, he clearly has issues."

"That's for the court to decide."

I sighed and leaned forward, placing my hands on the table. "If I talk, am I allowed to see him? Can I talk to him one last time?"

Detective Lawrence glanced at his partner and then looked back at me. "Of course. I can have that arranged. But I don't think it's a good idea seeing him now."

I frowned. "What do you mean by that? What's happening to him?"

"Look, Miss Grace," Detective Henry responded. "Caleb is a very cunning man. He's also a trickster. I have to admit that he had tried to talk one of our men into believing his innocence, and it almost worked. We don't want…"

"You don't want me to be fooled by him again. Isn't that why you're asking me not to see him?" I completed his statement.

"Yes, Miss Grace," that was Detective Lawrence. "It would be best if you stay out of Caleb's business for now. We just need your testimony on record and in court."

"He's not going to fool me again," I said to the detectives. "I can assure you of this, but I want to see him before all this ends. I need to ask him some questions."

Detective Lawrence nodded. "Alright, fine. I'll make arrangements for you to see him."

"Thank you," I appreciated.

He pushed the recorder closer to me. "So, are we ready?"

I gave them a smile. "Of course."

The evening of that day, Detective Lawrence brought me to see Caleb. He was being held in a cell several blocks from the department where I was interrogated.

I was searched thoroughly before I went inside. It wasn't like I was going to help Caleb escape, but the cops wanted to avoid anything like that. There was a high chance that even a victim of Caleb's was capable of freeing him.

When they brought Caleb to me, he had lost weight. He appeared thinner than the last time I saw him. His chin was also sprouting a stubble. As soon as he saw me, he broke down into tears and tried to hug me, but I wouldn't let him.

"You hate me." Those were the first words Caleb said when he took his seat.

"We all hate you," I replied. "Every woman you have hurt hates you."

He refused to look up at me. "I'm sorry."

I folded my arms and leaned back in my chair. "It's too late for that, isn't it? The court isn't going to hear your apologies. It would be focused on your crimes."

Then he raised his head to look at me. Caleb's eyes were misty. He couldn't even stop the tears from falling. I had never seen him this broken, trembling as though he could only feel fear. He knew that his life wasn't going to be the same.

"You're not testifying, are you?" Caleb asked.

I sighed and didn't reply. Detective Lawrence had told me not to tell him if I would be testifying or not. Caleb had his own defense lawyers. They would try to debunk my truth in every way possible.

Yeah, that's true. Caleb had his own team who would try to get him an acquittal. That was how justice worked. Even the vilest of men would be represented in court just to hear his own side of the story.

"You are," Caleb continued. "You're going to testify against me. How can you even do this to me?"

I slammed the desk with my palm. "What do you mean by that? I should be asking *you* why you did all those things to me."

"Because I love you," Caleb answered. "I still do. You need to understand this, Natalie. These people are trying to separate us. They don't want us to live our lives."

My eyebrows furrowed in confusion. "What people?"

He leaned forward and whispered, "The cops."

Damn, looking into his eyes, I could see how crazy he was. They were the gaze of a mad man. Why would anyone even think the cops' aim was to break our relationship? They had saved me from him. Everyone had warned me about Caleb, but it had taken me months to see the beast that I was battling with.

"No, they are not," I told him. "They are trying to save you, even if you don't like their methods."

"Save me?" he suddenly shouted.

The guard that was in the room glanced in our direction. I gestured at him that we were fine. Caleb didn't seem to notice that. He was enraged that I had spoken those words.

"They are not saving me, Natalie; neither are they saving you," Caleb continued. "They are going to make you hang me out to dry. You're going to be persuaded by them to send me to jail. I am innocent, Natalie. I didn't mean to hurt you. It wasn't my fault."

His words made me sick. Was Caleb really not sorry for what he did? Did he actually see himself as a guiltless man? How could he say all this after he beat me day after day? He even locked me up in a cabin and tried to drown me. The last thing he did was try to hold me captive in a dungeon, where he was also keeping his father and mother. How could he not understand his guilt?

"This is unbelievable," I said and rose to my feet. "You don't even feel sorry for what you did."

"Because I didn't do those things," Caleb insisted.

"So, who did it, Caleb?" I yelled, hearing my voice crack. I was about to cry. "Who fucking tried to drown me? Who hit me every time he had the chance to?"

Caleb rose to his feet and tried to touch me again. I gave him a hard stare, and he quickly backed away.

"You don't understand any of this, Natalie," Caleb said. "I couldn't control myself. It wasn't me. Someone else was controlling me."

"That's bullshit, Caleb," I said. "Extreme bullshit!"

"I wish you could understand me."

"I don't want to ever understand you," I answered. "Just because your dad fucked his sister doesn't mean I have to pay for his crimes."

That was when it happened again. Even with the possibility of jail term before him, Caleb couldn't control his temper. He came after me with sheer rage, but the guard stopped him, overpowering him and pinning his head to the table.

"Fuck you, Natalie! Fuck you! You have no right to talk about that!"

I shivered as they took me out of the room. Even as I left the room, I could still hear Caleb's curses. The realization that he could have hurt or killed me in that room made me extremely scared.

By the time Detective Lawrence got to me, I had stopped trembling. But there was a pain in my stomach; its cause I couldn't deduce. Yet, it made my head spin, and my vision blurry. It was almost as though I was about to lose consciousness. Had the fear of Caleb turned me into this? Was this the effect of having to live several horrible months with that man?

"Miss Grace, are you okay?" The detective was talking to me.

I raised my head. "No, I don't think so. I feel sick."

"It's okay." He was patting my shoulder. "I heard about what he tried to do. You're safe now. His outburst would only weaken his case."

"But I made him angry. I talked about his parents."

"His reaction was aberrant. Don't blame yourself."

There was no point in arguing for Caleb nor in blaming myself. Everyone had seen his abnormal behavior. Even without my testimony, Caleb would go to jail.

"I wanna go home," I said to him and stood up.

As soon as I did that, my sight twirled. I felt myself falling, just as a pair of arms grabbed me.

"Miss Grace?" I heard the detective say, but his voice sounded far away.

In no time, I had fallen to the ground, my eyes shutting to the darkness that overpowered me.

If Heaven smelled of antiseptics, it was indeed a place I wouldn't like to be in.

I flung my eyes open to an unfamiliar, white-washed ceiling, a throbbing ache on one side of my head. No one had to tell me I was in a hospital, and this wasn't Heaven.

I sat up slowly, trying to recollect what had happened. Oh, yes, I was at the police station, pulled away from an enraged Caleb, and then fell to the ground while Detective Lawrence held me in his arms. God! What had happened to me? It was funny how I just got out of one predicament that put me in a hospital, only to return to another one.

"You're awake?" A male nurse entered the room, bearing a warm smile.

All I could see was Caleb's face, the man who had broken me into pieces. The nurse looked like him for a split second. How could he have been so callous? How could he not have cared about me at all? I was sure that my loss of consciousness came from what he did to me. Caleb might be locked up in a cell, but he was still affecting my life.

"Miss Grace?" The nurse was calling my name.

"Ah, yes, I'm awake," I quickly replied, hoping he had not seen the sad look on my face.

"You've been out for five hours," the nurse began to explain, shuffling through a mess of papers in his hands.

"Just tell me where I am," I told him.

"The hospital. Don't you recognize it?"

That was when it hit me. I should have. The name was engraved into the wall of the hospital – D.E.M Medical Center. It was a place that I visited any time I got sick.

But I didn't want to spend much time here. Coming to the hospital always intensified my sickness. It reminded me of the day I ran from Caleb's cabin. This was the same hospital I ended up in.

"Uh, I have to go. I really do," I began to say, trying to get out of the hospital bed, but it was pointless.

The throbbing ache in my stomach increased with every muscle I moved. My eyes spun as the pain overwhelmed me, forcing me to grit my teeth and return to my previous position.

"You've got to relax, Miss Grace," the nurse informed me.

"What's wrong with me?" I asked.

Before he could reply, a familiar face entered the room. It was Dr. Meyers, the woman in charge, the director of the hospital. The pretty woman was also my doctor. She walked into the room, an apologetic smile on her face.

"I am so sorry, Natalie. Jim is an intern. He is not licensed to talk about your condition."

"It's okay, doctor," I answered.

Dr. Meyers came to check the drip passing through my vein.

"I've always told you to call me Melanie. How are you feeling?"

"There is this pain in my stomach that's making me swoon." That was my reply.

Dr. Meyers thought about this. "I'll have another doctor check you out before you leave." Then she turned to face Jim. "Tell Dr. Benson I'll be needing his help."

"Yes, doctor," Jim said before walking out of the room.

There was no way I was going to wait for another doctor to check me out. I needed to get out of here. Everything about this place reminded me of Caleb.

However, it was stupid walking out of here without knowing why I had collapsed. Obviously, something was wrong with me. If I didn't treat it now, I feared that I would be back here before I even reached the front door of my house.

Dr. Meyers would tell me everything. I needed to know if Caleb had done something to my body. No one had to tell me that this was because of him. I had gone through a lot, clinging to that man. The memories were overwhelming.

I tried hard not to cry in front of the doctor and said instead, "Isn't there anything I can take to reduce the pain? I really need to go back home."

"No," the doctor said firmly. "We need to know what's causing the pain."

I groaned, knowing it was of no use trying to talk Dr. Meyers out of this. She made the health of everyone her priority and would never discharge them until she was pretty sure they were okay.

"Fine, but I need to get out of here before night falls."

"I'll try to make that happen," Dr. Meyers said.

"Thanks."

"Uh, there's one more thing you should know, Natalie."

I looked at the doctor, and from the expression on her face, I knew she was about to tell me something I wouldn't like. How many times had I seen that look on the faces of doctors? They must have been trained to break bad news to their patients while keeping a calm face, but I knew how to look through them. It was the same thing Dr. Meyers was trying to do, but the pain that reflected in her eyes told me otherwise.

"What is it, doctor?" I asked calmly, bracing myself for what was coming next.

"Erm, you have been through a lot, Natalie, and you need to know that everything you went through had…it's more of a thing that…"

"Melanie," I called her name and gave her a hard stare. "What happened?"

"I'm really sorry to say this, Natalie, but you lost your baby."

What? Did she just say baby? Everything around me went spinning, and it wasn't because of the ache in my stomach. It was because I had now realized how fucked up my life was. I had a baby growing inside me? Now, it wasn't there anymore. Why was life this cruel? Why did it have to pick on me, to make me feel miserable?

"That's impossible," I said. "I'm not pregnant. I didn't feel…"

"Natalie," the doctor said, shaking her head. "You were three weeks pregnant. You wouldn't have known because your symptoms were in the early stages. But you did have a child, and a miscarriage happened when Caleb hurt you. I'm sorry."

Dr. Meyers was trying to console me. I didn't even know when I started to cry.

"My baby." Those words escaped my lips, shrouding me in absolute dejection that I would never be able to crawl out of. This was the end for me, and I knew it.

"Is that why I feel this pain?" I asked with quivering lips.

"Maybe," Dr. Meyers replied. "We can't be too sure. Another thing, Natalie. I hate to break this to you. I really hate it."

The doctor took my hand and squeezed it gently. Her horrible news was far from being done.

"You can't have a child ever again. You lost your womb. There was nothing we could do."

Months Later

I thought about many ways to die. You know, those painless ways to take my own life because there was no point staying in this world.

I mean, what would be my purpose? I had no one left to make me happy. Lauren tried her best to make me feel safe and loved. My father had finally taken time to talk to me and apologize for everything. Even my mother now took time to hang out with me and talk until it was dusk.

But they all couldn't fill this void in my life. Don't get me wrong. I wasn't depressed over the absence of Caleb in my life. Why would I care for a man who brought this emptiness into my world and seared these scars into my heart? Caleb was finally gone. The court had found him mentally unstable, and he would be living his life in a psychiatric ward for as long as the world stood.

But what about the misery he had brought upon me? If I had the chance to see Caleb again, it wouldn't be to chat with him. I would drive a dagger through his heart and make sure he bled to death.

The monster was responsible for the death of my baby. Each night, I put a hand on my stomach and thought about what the kid could have become. I would have trained him not to be like his father. I would have shown him love and made sure he didn't turn into a monster.

God! Why was I even thinking the baby was a boy? It could have been a girl. However, I wouldn't be able to find out its gender. It was gone forever.

See, there was one thing about losing a child and bearing hope that you would have another. Most women would cry over the miscarriage and just try to get pregnant again, making sure the baby stays. But this was impossible, in my case. I had lost my womb along with the baby. There was no way Natalie Grace would get to hold her baby in her arms ever again.

Now, you see why I wanted to die. If I couldn't bring a child into this world, then why stay in it? I had tried swallowing several pills that would knock me out or grant me a heart attack. But Lauren had walked in to save me. I begged her not to tell anyone about my suicidal attempt because it would mean sleeping in a ward in a mental facility. Why should I end up like Caleb McCord?

But the thoughts of killing myself refused to leave my head. As much as I tried to find hope in my dark world, I saw nothing. I just felt the emptiness, heard the silence, and saw the misery.

The day I tried to slit my wrist, I ate my last meal. It was my favorite meal, and I made sure to eat it to my satisfaction. There was no need in writing a letter. No one should know why I ended my life. Even my parents were unaware of the grandchild they lost. Only Lauren knew and Mr. Buckley. But they both talked about seeing happiness in other things and creating a great purpose to stay alive. They were both wrong. I didn't see any purpose to remain a living being. Whatever the world beyond had for me, I knew it was better than this place.

As soon as I took the last gulp of my wine, my phone began to ring. I groaned because I didn't want to speak to anyone before I died. Not even Lauren.

Yet, as I grabbed my phone and stared at the screen, something pulled me to pick it up. The first thing I heard was the sound of a woman crying.

"Hello?" I spoke.

"Is this Natalie Grace?" the sobbing woman asked.

"Yes. Who is this?" I asked in return.

"I am Ellie Marigold," she told me. "Please, you have to help me."

I was surprised that a woman like her was asking me for help. Of course, everyone knew Ellie Marigold. She was a popular on-screen actress whose romantic life with her boyfriend, Bruce Hills, was the talk of the town. Everyone appreciated their love. They were the example of a perfect love.

"Miss Marigold?" I said, rising to my feet. "How did you get this number?"

"I watched you testify against Caleb McCord, and I have to admit that you're a brave woman. Going through all of that, and you saved yourself."

Somehow, I feared that I knew why Miss Marigold wanted my help. Could it be…?

"How can I help you?"

"My story is just like yours, Natalie," Ellie said. "Bruce won't let me go, but he keeps hurting me. I need you to save me. You need to save my best friend, too. She is in an abusive relationship. We need you, Natalie. Help us."

At that point, I began to see my purpose. No, the next thing wasn't to take my own life. I should stay in this world and help others who had gone through hell like me.

As I dropped the phone after promising Ellie we would talk tomorrow morning, I smiled to myself and discarded the knife that I would have used to cut myself.

I was a winner. I had to make others win, too. Even if it meant staying alive and remembering that I was barren, I would not stop. There were a lot of people who needed to be rescued.

Forever Yours

Forever Yours

Forever Yours

www.ingramcontent.com/pod-product-compliance
Lightning Source LLC
Chambersburg PA
CBHW060859190726
48286CB00002B/300